THE LEGEND OF GOOD WOMEN

THE LEGEND OF
Good Women

BY GEOFFREY CHAUCER

TRANSLATED BY ANN McMILLAN

RICE UNIVERSITY PRESS

HOUSTON

First Edition, 1987

Requests for permission to reproduce material

from this work should be addressed to:

Rice University Press

Post Office Box 1892

Houston, Texas 77251

Library of Congress Cataloging in Publication Data

Chaucer, Geoffrey, d. 1400.

The legend of good women.

Includes bibliographies and index.

1. Women—Poetry. 2. Women—Mythology—Poetry.

3. Women—Biography—Poetry. I. McMillan, Ann,

1952–   II. Title.

PR 1881.M36   1987   821'.1   86-60780

ISBN 0-89263-261-5

ISBN 0-89263-264-X (pbk.)

CONTENTS

ILLUSTRATIONS

PREFACE

This translation is intended to make Chaucer's *Legend of Good Women* more easily accessible to readers who are reluctant to attempt his Middle English verse. It is particularly aimed at those who are interested in what Marina Warner calls "the taxonomy of female types," for the *Legend* is concerned with one of the most frequently encountered and most vexing of those types: the woman destroyed by love.

The introduction presents my own understanding of what the *Legend* means; this understanding, in turn, shapes my translation. A translator does her best to approximate what the author meant, but her own interpretation determines not only the choice of one word over another but also the overall tone of the translated work. My belief that the *Legend* is ironic in its praise for martyrs of love inevitably colors my representation of Chaucer. For this reason, I urge those who wish to make a serious study of the *Legend* to read it in Middle English. The subtleties of meaning, as well as the sound of the verse, cannot be fully reproduced.

I have tried to keep this translation as literal as possible, following Chaucer in his frequent shifting of pronouns and verb tense. Though these shifts may be puzzling at first, they carry a dramatic value without which the poem would be less effective.

I want to thank E. Talbot Donaldson for his careful reading of the translation. Joe Beatty was a most perspicacious reader of the introduction. Thanks also to Carl Lindahl, Charlotte Fitzgerald, Julian Wasserman, and John Fisher.

PART I

INTRODUCTION

CHAUCER AND THE LEGEND

OF GOOD WOMEN

G eoffrey Chaucer wrote *The Legend of Good Women* in 1386, between *Troilus and Criseyde* and *The Canterbury Tales*. The "legend" of the title plays upon the medieval term for a work chronicling
the lives of saints.[1] The term thus implies not fiction but truth, as revealed in the stories of the Christian martyrs. In Chaucer's work, however, the "martyrs" are women from classical mythology and history
who suffered and died for love. Their lovers, as agents of their martyrdom, fill the roles that Christian legends usually reserve for Roman
emperors. Women who are destroyed by love, but remain faithful, join
the ranks of Cupid's martyrs in a Paradise made up entirely of women.

Chaucer's *Legend* comprises nine individual legends, one with two
separate sections, introduced by a long prologue that exists in two versions. Although the stories and their heroines differ greatly from one
another in their classical sources, Chaucer's retellings have a formulaic
quality: women are innocent victims, men vicious deceivers. Chaucer
left the work unfinished; it breaks off near the end of a legend, and
internal evidence suggests that he had planned more.[2] The *Legend* represents Chaucer's first extended use of the decasyllabic couplet form in
which most of the *Canterbury Tales* are written. Because of its position
in the canon, its rhyme scheme, its use of a prologue and collection of
stories, and its abrupt ending, some think that the *Legend* was put
aside by Chaucer when a better idea came to him: the similarly arranged but very different *Canterbury Tales*.

The notion that Chaucer could not bring himself to finish the *Legend* has some internal corroboration. The prologue depicts Chaucer's
narrator[3] as being forced to write stories of good women as penance
for having angered the God of Love.[4] Within the legends themselves,
Chaucer repeatedly makes such comments as "I would tell the whole
story, but it would take too much time" and "Her sufferings were so
great that I can hardly bear to tell you about them, so I will be brief."
This sense of expediency and distaste contributes importantly to the
characterization of the narrator and to the theme. In the early part of

this century, however, critics accepted this pose of ennui as autobiographical fact.[5]

In part because of what was taken to be Chaucer's own boredom with the *Legend*, it has until recently been accorded very little critical attention. For years its theme and execution appeared so easily apprehended that few scholars found it worthy of comment. The theme is indeed straightforward and is stated with merciless repetition. Women possess more virtue than men; the proof lies in the fact that women suffer more in love. In the *Legend*'s prologue, the God of Love dictates praise of women because they are more "true and kind" in love than men—both by their nature as women and by their conscious dedication to the ideal of chaste love. The *Legend* exalts women as martyrs to their sex and to the ideal—chastity—that was deemed crucial to it.

In the *Legend*, Chaucer includes Lucrece and Thisbe, chaste women who are often depicted as the innocent victims of malign fate. He also includes Cleopatra and Medea, who are usually treated as anything but innocent. Murder, incest, infanticide, and adultery speckle the careers of these women, and even the best are not above criticism for their deeds. Yet Chaucer omits these notorious details. All his "good women" are equally innocent and equally victims. Whether she adheres to the ideal of chastity, barters it for a promise of love, or forsakes it altogether, the "good woman" of the *Legend* ends by being sacrificed to it.

As long as one focuses on the supposed quaintness of the *Legend*, its incongruities may be dismissed merely as evidence of fuzzy medieval thinking. As early as 1909, however, Harold C. Goddard suggested that the *Legend* may be deliberately funny in exalting Medea alongside Thisbe as a martyr of love.[6] John Livingston Lowes rebutted him so forcefully that almost fifty years elapsed before the argument was made again.[7]

In the 1960s two important works drew attention to the irony of the *Legend* and to the implications of its message about women. Eleanor Winsor Leach's dissertation, "The Sources and Rhetoric of Chaucer's 'Legend of Good Women' and Ovid's 'Heroides,'"[8] sees both poets as mocking the heroines they pretend to exalt. Pat Trefzger Overbeck's article "Chaucer's Good Woman"[9] explores the links between the women of the *Legend* and women in other works by Chaucer. Some recent interpretations of the *Legend* have moved away from its announced subject—that is, women and their sufferings—to explore the poem's use of symbols related to religious faith [10] and to poetry itself. [11] Still others are approaching the *Legend* with some of the tools of feminist criticism. While their work is in progress, it is already yielding results that will inspire rereading and debate for a long time to come. Elaine Hansen, Sheila Delany, and Arlyn Diamond, for example, are among those whose recent work on the *Legend* has taken at least a point of departure from feminist criticism. [12] Yet the *Legend* is far from exhausted in what it has to tell us about women and about romantic love. Chaste, self-sacrificing love as the highest ideal for women is neither an immutable truth nor a remotely picturesque literary convention, but a powerful myth [13] to which our culture has given shape and that in turn shapes our culture and its individual members.

The ideal, its representatives, and its chroniclers go back many centuries before Chaucer and have continued to proliferate long after his day. Vergil, Ovid, Boccaccio, and other classical and medieval writers composed works in which many of the same characters appear as examples of women who succeeded or failed in attaining the ideal. Each of the groupings (called "catalogues") achieves its thematic unity and significance, stated or unstated, by using the familiar figures of exemplary women to make a point about women in general. Different authors treat the same women very differently, however. Vergil's martyrs to passionate self-loss in *Aeneid* VI and Boccaccio's self-sacrificing wives in *De Claris Mulieribus* (*Concerning Famous Women*) may not appear to have much in common with each other or with the women of Chaucer's *Legend*. Although they are indeed different from one another in almost every way, all these women at last assume the role of sexual victim.

This role does have factual, objective content in the "taxonomy of female types." [14] Women can be overpowered, raped; pregnancy can expose them as unchaste. Beyond these facts, however, women are victims of subtler forces. The women of Vergil, Ovid, Boccaccio, and Chaucer may be good or bad in many senses, but all are victims of the belief that chastity is their only possible virtue, the only source of whatever value they have in society's eyes and their own.

To say that chastity is the crucial virtue for medieval women is certainly no exaggeration. For example, Saint Jerome in *Epistola Adversus Jovinianum* says, "a woman's only virtue is chastity"—*mulieris virtus proprie pudicitia est*. [15] Christine de Pizan calls it "the supreme virtue in women," the virtue without which "all their others would be nothing."[16] Philippe de Navarre, Giovanni Boccaccio, and countless others echo this belief. Cupid himself makes clear his own concern with chastity in his references to "clean maidens, true wives, and steadfast widows" ("G" Prologue, lines 282–283) as the proper subjects of Chaucer's legends.

The story of Dido, which Chaucer tells in *The House of Fame* and again in the *Legend*, offers an instructive example of the role of chastity. In these two works and in his sources, Vergil and Ovid, it is clear that excessive passion betrays Dido to her fate, but that what actually destroys her is the loss of her chaste reputation. Her story will be discussed later, but its thematic importance is so great that it deserves mention here.

Dido, a widow, was founder and ruler of Carthage. She clung to her vow of chaste widowhood and rejected offers of marriage from neighboring kings, Iarbus among them. When Aeneas, fleeing Troy at its fall, came to her for aid, she broke this vow; they became lovers. When he left her to follow his destiny as founder of Rome, she killed herself. The four accounts mentioned above depict her as committing suicide not out of thwarted passion, but out of the certainty that she would no longer be permitted to live and reign as before.

Vergil's Dido tells Aeneas, "Because of you the tribes of Libya, all the Nomad princes hate me, even my own Tyrians are hostile; and for you my honor is gone and that good name that once was mine."[17] The word here translated as "honor" is *pudor*.[18] The word also means "shame" and is related to *pudendum* (literally, "that of which one should be ashamed"), a scholarly euphemism for a woman's external sexual organs. In the passages here quoted from Vergil and Ovid, as well as in many others, *pudor* and *fama*—"fame," but also "infamy"—appear together repeatedly. They force the reader to realize how public the consequences of private sexual shame are for Dido.[19]

"Why do I live on," she continues, ". . . until Iarbus . . . takes me prisoner?" (*Aeneid,* Mandelbaum translation, p. 92). Later she asks herself, "What can I do? Shall I . . . go back again to my old suitors, begging, seeking a wedding with Numidians whom I have already often scorned as bridegrooms?" And she laments, "I have not held fast the faith I swore before the ashes of my Sychaeus" (ibid., pp. 99–100).

Ovid's Dido, in *Heroides* VII, begins her letter to Aeneas by saying that she has lost "desert, . . . reputation and . . . purity of body and

FIGURE 1. Dido. By permission of Bodleian Library, Oxford.

soul" (p. 83) by becoming his lover. The letter is filled with references to her lost reputation, to the shame she feels that the story of their union is known, and to her fear for the consequences of her infamy. "Why do you not bind me forthwith, and give me over to Gaetulian Iarbus?" she asks Aeneas (*Heroides* VII, p. 93).

Dido in Chaucer's *House of Fame* shows particular awareness of the double standard. Every man, she says, will have a new love—or three: one to enhance his reputation, one for friendship, and one for pleasure or profit (lines 301–310). *Her* reputation, however, is destroyed by "wicked Fame": "though I might live forever, I would never recover from what I have done, so that I would not be said to have been shamed by Aeneas. And I shall be judged thus: 'Lo, as she has done before, she will do again'—this is what people say among themselves" (lines 349, 353–359).

Each of these Didos expresses despair not at a future without love, but at a future in which infamy makes her unable to protect her country and her person from the next powerful man to covet it and her. The *Legend*'s Dido states her vision of her fate even more plainly. She begs Aeneas, "Have mercy! Let me with you ride! / The lords of all these lands on every side / Will soon destroy me, solely for your sake" (lines

1317–1318). Seen in the context of these speeches, Dido's suicide is not solely a tragic act of excessive passion, although passion sets the machinery in motion. Her suicide is depicted as an attempt to escape the destruction that will follow her loss of chaste reputation.

In idealized literary depictions such as romance novels,[20] a woman's chaste love wins her the protection of a man who values it and her; loving him becomes her highest goal. Dido's story, as it is told by Vergil, Ovid, and Chaucer (as well as others not mentioned here), illustrates the failure of the ideal. Dido gives her chastity to Aeneas expecting a return that does not materialize. For the other "good women" of the *Legend* as well, this ideal carries a high price. Many of the "good women" barter their chastity for a false assurance of love; when it fails them, the ideal of chastity requires that they kill themselves rather than live with an evil name. Even those who remain chaste find that they must sacrifice themselves for their husbands or lovers, or for their own reputations. The *Legend* shows the ideal of chastity not as protecting women but as making them more vulnerable.

The theme of women's victimization in the *Legend* has great significance for other works by Chaucer. The fates of its "good women" tell us much not only about Dido's dilemma in *The House of Fame,* but about Criseyde's in *Troilus and Criseyde* and Dorigen's in *The Franklin's Tale.* All these heroines confront the double standard that threatens death or shame to women who violate the ideal of chaste, faithful love. Their fear of being (or of being known as) unchaste leads all these women to commit, or at least contemplate, suicide. Chaucer begins his characterization of the Wife of Bath by having her refute the doctrine of chaste love in a way that shows her intimate acquaintance with that doctrine. Through its assessment of the rules governing romantic relations between men and women and of the rules governing poets who write about them, the *Legend* has important implications for many of Chaucer's other works.

This essay seeks to provide background and commentary on the *Legend* in a useful, cogent form. The first section discusses the beginnings of the catalogue tradition, giving particular attention to the classical catalogues of Ovid and Vergil and to an influential early medieval catalogue by Saint Jerome. The second discusses the medieval catalogue of women as written by Chaucer's contemporaries, especially Boccaccio and Christine de Pizan. These writers try to define women's virtue by example, and their attempts illustrate their different attitudes toward women's moral nature.

Chaucer follows Ovid and Vergil in not differentiating between "good" and "bad" women, as Boccaccio and Christine are careful to do. He complicates the issue, however, by trying to make a diverse collection of women fit the pattern of the saint's life and the ideal of chaste love. In so doing, Chaucer deliberately combines (and confuses) classical and medieval traditions to achieve ironic tension and distortion in the voice of his narrator. The third section shows how this narrative voice is developed in the *Legend*'s prologue. The fourth section discusses the techniques that Chaucer uses in the legends themselves to convey the sense of distorted communication in a narrator forced to follow the demands of two incompatible traditions. Finally, a brief consideration of *The Franklin's Tale* and the prologue to *The Wife of Bath's Tale* shows how their heroines view themselves in terms of the ideal of chaste love.

Chaucer's method and purpose in the *Legend* do not lend themselves to neat summary. Those who have found historical references, religious symbols, discussions of poetic truth, and much more are doubtless quite correct in doing so, for Chaucer was adept at weaving many threads of meaning and suggestion into his works. This introduction takes as its thesis the belief that Chaucer's *Legend* is concerned with the process by which a rigid ideal destroys women's individual differences and forces them to embrace their own victimization. He undermines the pernicious praise of women as victims by inflating that praise past reasonable bounds, by applying it to inappropriate and vitiated figures, by undercutting the ideals themselves, and by creating a narrator so unwilling to write the assigned work that his trustworthiness is suspect from the beginning.

ORIGINS AND DEVELOPMENT OF THE CATALOGUE TRADITION

In the prologue to Chaucer's *Legend*, the God of Love asserts to the doubting narrator that old books tell the stories of a hundred good women for every bad one. When Cupid calls to witness "God, and all the clerks," we have reason to suspect irony on Chaucer's part. Medieval clerks (clerics, scholars in clerical orders) epitomize those men in all ages who believe that the life of the spirit demands rejection of the body. The writings of these clerks depict women as enemies allied to the flesh. Virtually every medieval author, clerk or not, wrote at least one work of antifeminist satire following classical and Christian models.

When Cupid goes on to name Ovid and Saint Jerome as writers who praise women, the irony deepens. Ovid details the art of seducing women and escaping the consequences in his *Ars Amatoria;* Saint Jerome preaches the abhorrence of women's charms. This passage alerts the reader to Chaucer's humorous intent in the *Legend.* Yet complexities remain, for the God of Love is not simply mistaking the facts, although he is distorting them.

The literary treatment of women from the very earliest times has produced a tangle of paradoxes. Attempts to show women as evil often dwell on repulsive details of sexuality and childbirth. In order not to underestimate the enemy's strength, however, writers also portray women as almost irresistibly attractive. The resulting creature exhibits great powers of both attraction and repulsion. She appears emblematically in the story, often depicted in medieval art, of a demon who takes the shape of a beautiful woman in order to tempt a holy man (sometimes Saint Anthony). He dispels the charm by raising the hem of her gown to show the hideous tail concealed beneath it.

Given this notion of female sexuality, it is not surprising to find that the praise of women dwells chiefly on virgins and chaste wives. To the clerks, a chaste woman was an enemy disarmed. But the other kinds of women who receive praise surprise us more—at least at first. Manly women attain the ranks of the good, based on the fact that the word *virtue* comes from *vir,* "man." A virtuous woman is she who least resembles her own inferior sex. Amazons and warrior-queens thus enter the lists of the good. A third type of praise takes the assumption that "chastity is a woman's only virtue" and turns it around. It reasons that because chastity offers women their only possible worth in the eyes of men, they must invest it very carefully in men who will remain faithful to them; the men themselves suffer no such constraint. Women therefore attain the "virtue" of suffering more in love than men do, since their choice of whether or not to love, and of whom to love, is the most important decision of their lives. Women betrayed by their lovers thus sometimes come under the heading of good women, even though their behavior may not be virginal or chaste in the strictest sense.[21]

A collection of virgins and manly women, used to contrast with the majority of their sex, appears in Jerome's tract *Adversus Jovinianum,* mentioned above. The work argues in favor of priestly celibacy and celibacy in general by portraying sexually active women and marriage as repellent. Ovid's *Heroides* tells the stories of women suffering in love from the women's point of view. Some are traditionally good (Penelope), some bad (Helen); but Ovid's treatment of them is sympathetic, at least at face value. Thus, these authors can be said to tell the stories of "good women," just as the God of Love claims. The questions do not end there, however. The jumble of contradictions found in medieval defenses of women yields no neat resolution. Perhaps the discrepancies between what the authors themselves wanted in women, what the Church told them they ought to admire in women, and what experience taught them they could find in women remained irreconcilable.

THE CATALOGUE DEVICE

The catalogue, by Utley's definition, is a "compilation of examples, which makes its appeal not to logic but to symbolism."[22] These compilations range in length from a few lines—really just a list of names—to hundreds of pages. Because of the allusive nature of the catalogue, the names and stories had to be familiar. Almost all the women used as examples come from classical mythology and history. Medieval readers could find these heroines not only in classical sources, especially Ovid and Vergil, but also in popular medieval authors, including Saint Jerome, John of Salisbury, Jean de Meun, Boccaccio, Jean LeFevre, Eustace Deschamps, Christine de Pizan, John Gower, Dante, and Chaucer himself. In most of these works the *Legend*'s "good women" appear as bad examples, so that more shocking elements of their stories would have been well known.

Brief catalogues most often contain not rhetoric unrelated to the work that encloses them, but the isolation and exploration of important themes. Long catalogues that stand by themselves, as the *Legend* does, form their own unity by interweaving repeated themes. As a result, they construct a whole in which each part gains by association with the others. In composing catalogues of women, authors play with their audiences' assumptions and reveal their own; these works can throw unexpected light upon shadowy areas of women's history. They can also deepen our understanding of medieval authors' attitudes toward their sources. Scholars have sometimes asserted the dependence of medieval writers upon established "authority"—finding evidence, for example, in Chaucer's claim in the *Legend* that he is following old books. Yet no authorities contradict each other or themselves more often than those telling the stories of exemplary women, as Chaucer's *Legend* demonstrates. In the very act of using or citing authorities such as Vergil, Ovid, and Saint Jerome, he is often undermining the whole notion of transmitted truth and poetic authority.

CLASSICAL HEROINES

Agamemnon, using the examples of Clytemnestra and Helen, warned Odysseus in the underworld not to trust Penelope. He was helping set a precedent that would be followed for more than two thousand years. Most classical catalogues of women warned men to beware of them. There were a few exceptions—praise for chaste wives as rare treasures, or for consecrated virgins as links between the human and divine. In the earliest extant catalogues, by Homer and Hesiod, we find the roots of this tradition. Hesiod's *Catalogue of Women* survives only in fragments. It was "a series of genealogies which traced the Hellenic race . . . from a common ancestor. The reason why women are so prominent is obvious: since most families and tribes claimed to be descended from a god, the only safe clue to their origins was through the mortal woman beloved by that god." [23] The women receive praise for their beauty, their union with gods, and their famous offspring.

Homer's catalogue of the women whom Odysseus sees in Hades, "consorts or daughters of illustrious men," [24] begins by emphasizing the same attributes. Odysseus speaks to his host, Alkínoös, of the women he saw: Tyro, Antiope, Alkmene, and others appear, with the stories of their fateful loves. Then Odysseus turns to "[o]ther and sadder tales . . . of some who came through all the Trojan spears . . . only to find a brutal death at home—and a bad wife behind it" (*Odyssey*, p. 197). Odysseus then recounts the stories of Clytemnestra and Helen. The shade of Agamemnon reveals his murder at the hands of his wife and her lover. Odysseus responds, "Myriads died by Helen's fault, and [Clytemnestra] plotted against you half the world away" (p. 199). Agamemnon warns Odysseus by these examples to "[i]ndulge a woman never, and never tell her all you know" (p. 199), for "the day of faithful wives is gone forever" (*Odyssey*, p. 200).

This sweeping condemnation of women loses something of its force in context. Before speaking with Agamemnon in Hades, Odysseus has already been assured by his mother's shade that Penelope remains faithful. And when Odysseus tells the story to Alkínoös and his court, the "wise and virtuous" queen Arêtê is present as an example to the contrary. This catalogue of women, good and bad (but mostly bad), functions less as a convincing indictment of women than as a statement of their inescapable importance. In the world of Homer and Hesiod, a man's choice of wife could literally be a matter of life and death. If he went away to war for a long time, she gained at least some measure of control over his property. Unchastity might lead to deceit, theft, murder, or to the passing of a man's property into the hands of bastards. A good wife was a man's most important investment, for which the culturally enforced ideal of chastity functioned as a sort of guarantee.

The destructive energy that women like Clytemnestra bring to their "unchastity" is pictured as abhorrent in these early Greek catalogues. It remained for the great dramatists—Aeschylus, Sophocles, and especially Euripides—to exalt these women's passion to tragic grandeur. Moreover, these dramatists show women's unchastity as resulting not from lust but from their determination to punish their husbands in the most horrible ways available to them. Clytemnestra takes a lover, then plots with him to kill her husband, in order to avenge Agamemnon's sacrifice of their daughter.[25] This and other stories indicate a close link between women's unchastity and their rebellion against what society takes to be the husband's and father's rights over his wife and family.

For the purposes of the medieval catalogue tradition, however, exalted passion becomes associated with women through Ovid and Vergil. Vergil's catalogue of women in Hades is based upon Odysseus' encounter with the shades of famous women. The catalogue, only five lines long, names the women with Dido in the "sorrowing fields," *Lugentes Campi*.[26] Ovid's *Heroides* purport to be "letters from legendary women to absent husbands or lovers."[27] The whole collection runs to about three thousand lines. It may seem to be stretching a point to give such different works the same classification, but the similarities are more significant. Both catalogues list a group of famous women with some reference to their stories; they play upon the reader's knowledge of the stories to achieve their desired effects; and they perpetuate the same notions about women.

Vergil's catalogue, although very short, has a special importance for our purposes here. The whole conception of the *Legend*—a Paradise of women who died for love—bears great resemblance to Vergil's catalogue of women in Hades who were destroyed by passion. In Book VI of the *Aeneid,* Dido—now in Hades—is seen one last time by Aeneas. Dido's shade is described in terms that recall her reactions to Aeneas's leave-taking in Book IV: then she was "turned away," "rolling her eyes," "with silent eyes," "enflamed" (*Aeneid* IV, lines 362–364, p. 85). She vowed vengeance but, breaking off, turned from his eyes and from the light of day (*Aeneid* IV, lines 388–389, p. 86). As a shade, she is still "burning," still avoiding his eyes, still silent (*Aeneid* VI, lines 467–471, p. 139). These verbal echoes suggest that even in death Dido exists suspended in the moment of Aeneas' desertion. The references to "burning" show that both love [28] and hate continue. They also recall the moment of her death, when she set fire to the belongings left by Aeneas and threw herself into the flames. In Hades she dwells in the "secret places" and "myrtle wood" (myrtle sacred to the dead and to Venus). These attributes of the sorrowing fields suggest that her confinement there is not so much a punishment as a continuation of her own choice in life, a projection of her emotional state.

With Dido is a group of women "whom harsh love destroyed with cruel ruin" (*Aeneid* VI, line 442, p. 138). As Jaques Perret observes, "the group of heroines which accompanies Dido in Hades was not composed without design." [29] Traditionally, three—Phaedra, Eriphyle, and Pasiphae—are gross offenders against nature. Pasiphae, for example, copulated with a bull and gave birth to the Minotaur. Three—Procris, Evadne, and Laodamia—are innocent victims of love; Laodamia killed herself rather than survive her husband's death. In the larger context that Perret sees at work, however, all these women are "victims in part voluntary of the most pitiable, perhaps, but also the most damnable error"; they allowed passion to destroy them (Perret, p. 257).

The last of the group, Caenis, is a figure who comments powerfully on the group as a whole and on the characterization of Dido. Caenis, according to the stories, was changed from a woman to a man during his lifetime; only in the *Aeneid* has his form changed back to female in Hades. Perret sees this double metamorphosis as "the projection or representation on a physical plane of what was, on the moral plane, the destiny of Dido." He traces the transformation of Dido from "the tender virgin given in marriage to Sychaeus" to "a leader (*dux femina facti*)" carrying out the masculine role of city-building; to, in Hades, a "young girl" once more united with the husband of her youth (Perret, p. 252).

According to Ovid, Caenis is a beautiful maiden who wishes to remain a virgin but is overpowered by Neptune. In response to his promise to grant her anything she wanted, she replies, "This injury calls forth the great desire that I be unable to suffer so again; grant to me that I no longer be a woman; you will have given me all." [30] Caenis is a victim of rape, and she chooses never again to be a victim, although the choice means rejecting her own sex. After death she returns not only to her sex but also to the pattern of woman as victim symbolized in the sorrowing fields. Her double transformation represents the plight of women trapped in their sex and in the limitations of its roles. That Caenis becomes a woman again after her death underscores the temporary nature of Dido's escape from her sex. It also seems to deflect some of the blame put on the women themselves and to place it upon the inexorable pattern of sexual roles. Dido, like Caenis, transcends her sex and performs a male role, and her escape from sexual constraints is likewise limited. Her masculine freedom depends upon her adherence to the essential female code, for it is based on her status as a chaste widow. Her fall from an independent male role to that of woman as victim is, like that of Caenis, unforeseen and precipitous.

The physical description of the sorrowing fields emphasizes the particular qualities of this distinctively female suffering. Unlike the men in Tartarus, the women suffer pain more emotional than physical. The place is secretive, shameful, dark, devoted to mourning and self-absorption. This sense of shamefulness and concealment is echoed in Dido's own appearance and behavior. She cannot meet Aeneas's eyes; her rage at him seems mingled with self-loathing. Finally, she runs to join her husband Sychaeus. Their reunion in Hades has not healed her; her wound still bleeds, and her burning continues. The fact that Sychaeus shares her grief does not seem to diminish it but maintains it, as if she were dwelling on the same wrong for eternity. The sorrowing fields contain all the women Aeneas sees in Hades; there are none in Tartarus or the Elysian fields. The two living women mentioned in this section of the poem, Helen and Clytemnestra, are surely to be seen as bound for its dark pathways after their deaths.

Vergil's use of this catalogue associates Dido with other women whose stories say something about the nature of love. Some of them have been considered good, some evil. Vergil does not state judgment; he lets their appearance together suggest that they represent varying aspects of the same flawed passion—a passion characteristic of women. Medieval authors adapted this use of the catalogue for characterization and illustration. They also adapted its message about women though, unlike Vergil, they rarely refrained from stating moral judgments.

Ovid also presents the stories of women wronged by love and provides no external moral framework. With Vergil's catalogue, Ovid's *Heroides* is the most significant source for Chaucer's *Legend*. The stories told in the *Heroides* were all familiar to Ovid's contemporaries; the reader knew the outcome and the "true" circumstances, while the women, at the imagined moment of composing their letters, did not. Howard Jacobson points out that this discrepancy between impersonal myth and first-person narrative brings about a "duality" between "'objective' events and individual perspective."[31] Ovid does not so much alter the "facts" of the story as distort them through the emotional perspectives of the women involved. In reading the accusations of Penelope against Odysseus, for example, we feel the shock of seeing a familiar situation from an unfamiliar vantage point. In this supposed archetype of the faithful, patient wife, we see love alternating with rage and self-righteousness with suspicion. Penelope recalls her fears during the siege of Troy, relives the moments of reunion granted to other wives, regrets the end of the war ("at least I knew where you were"),[32] imagines Odysseus mocking her lack of sophistication to amuse a new lover. The faithful Penelope of Homer is here an angry and bitter woman, well aware that those who have told the story have not consulted her feelings in the matter.

Dido's letter to Aeneas, which greatly influenced medieval retellings of their story, makes a strong first-person statement of those forces within Dido that Vergil shows primarily from the outside. Ovid's Dido "burns," too, in the strength of her conflicting emotions. The letter begins with an admission that all hope is lost, so that "to lose words is light" (*Heroides* VII, line 6, p. 82). The struggle of hope against despair persists throughout the letter, however, as does the conflict between pride and self-abasement. Pride speaks in words of love ("I . . . began our love, and do not feel ashamed for it" (VII, line 33, p. 83) and of near-hate ("live, I pray . . . you shall the better be known as the cause of my death" [VII, lines 63–64, p. 86]). Then come moments of self-abnegation to deflate pride, as when she says she is not worth enough for Aeneas to risk his life fleeing her, or when she accepts the penalty demanded by shame (*pudor,* VII, line 97, p. 90). In her last plea to make him stay, she combines pride and humility in offering her wealth, her city, herself—if not as bride, then as whatever he will accept: "so long as she is yours, Dido will endure to be what you wish" (VII, line 168, p. 96). Ovid's treatment of Dido does not differ from Vergil's in the facts; but by undercutting her pride and rage with futile pleading, Ovid makes his heroine much more pathetic. Yet Ovid's letter greatly resembles Vergil's sorrowing fields in that it traps Dido at her weakest moment—the moment in which she realizes that she has let passion destroy her.

This anguished shifting from one state of mind to another—sometimes rational and cunning, sometimes emotional and self-defeating—persists throughout the *Heroides.* Whether the speaker is maiden, wife, widow, or illicit lover, and whether or not she has grounds for complaint, she shows the characteristic frenzied helplessness. Revealingly, this extreme emotionalism is so closely associated with women in literature and in life that the *Heroides* "are not rarely praised as acute portraits of the female psyche" (Jacobson, p. 371). In discussing this supposed psychological realism, Jacobson observes that these "powerless women who are helpless to influence their own lives must resort to vicarious (and futile) acts to provide psychic satisfaction in the absence of potency, be it weeping, complaining, or verbal expression" (Jacobson, p. 372).

The women's powerlessness in matters of love and sex qualifies them for the sorrowing fields and the *Heroides.* This helplessness, however, does not exist in isolation; it is the result of an almost complete lack of self-determination in any area of life. The families, friends, nations, and even enemies of these women devote much time and trouble to making their choices for them. Penelope must use all her cunning to avoid a forced marriage with one of her importunate suitors. Dido walks a tightrope; she can live freely, though precariously, as long as she does not lapse from her vow of chastity. No wonder that the question of whether or not to love becomes an obsession for the women themselves. It is the only question anyone ever asks about them, the only thing they are expected to do—or not to do. Women are victims not only of men's untrustworthiness and society's constraints but also of their own conflicting and finally overwhelming emotions.

The poetic treatments of these women tend to evoke pity mixed with contempt. The "reduction of great, sometimes cataclysmic, events and myths [such as the Trojan War] to the narrow egocentric world of the heroine" (Jacobson, p. 352) makes the Ovidian complaints seem at times petty and hysterical. (The word *hysterical,* from the Greek word for *uterus,* was invented to name this type of "characteristically female" behavior.)

How does Ovid mean for his readers to react to his heroines? Eleanor Winsor Leach sees Ovid's characterizations as mocking the Augustan values—"loyalty," "simplicity," "good faith"—of which they are extreme, perhaps perverse, examples. She points to Ovid's own condemnation of some of the same women in his *Ars Amatoria:* "What will destroy you, I will tell you; you have not learned how to love; / the art has failed in you; love survives by art." Leach goes on to say that the women "boast of their loyalty, their simplicity, and their confidence; and . . . put their lovers ethically in the wrong." [33] If loyalty, simplicity, and so on—all components of the ideal of chastity—are coins with which to purchase love, the women are right to feel cheated. But if these virtues are their own reward, or are gifts freely given, the women are invalidating their claims to virtue in the very act of making such claims.

The *Heroides* themselves, however, contain no statement of how they are to be read. Ovid's medieval audience, unless they remembered the *Ars Amatoria,* were free to make their own conclusions and to put his material to their own uses. Some medieval writers appear to have sympathized with the women more than Ovid himself may have done. Yet, of course, this very sympathy implies willingness to believe in women's inherent weakness and emotionalism. Vergil's and Ovid's catalogues popularized an idea of women as over-emotional and dependent on men. They also showed that women's position in society helps to make them so. The degree to which medieval writers assimilated the latter idea varied widely.

SAINT JEROME

Catalogues by early Christian writers tended, predictably, to focus on bad women. Katharine M. Rogers states that "every one of the major Christian writers from the first century through the sixth assumed the mental and moral frailty of women." [34]

Saint Jerome's catalogue of virtuous pagan women seems at first to be an exception. But this work, which refutes Jovinian's claim that chaste married people are equal to virgins in the sight of God, really defends not women but virginity. Jerome first argues the superiority of virginity to marriage with examples, mostly male, from the Old and New Testaments. He then attempts to prove that virginity is not an unnatural state imposed by overly rigorous Christians but was honored among pagans as well. His examples from Greek and Roman myth and history, unlike those from the Bible, are all female. This fact does not indicate any special reverence for women. First of all, he is limited by his sources. As Sarah B. Pomeroy observes, "[a]mong the [Greek and Roman] gods there are no virgins. . . . In contrast, three of the five Olympian goddesses are virgins." [35] Among mythological mortals, too, he would find virginity in men treated as a temporary state or an unnatural one, as in the cases of Hippolytus, Narcissus, and Hermaphrodite. Since Jerome does sometimes bend his "facts" to further his argument, the mere scarcity of virginal men does not completely explain his tactics here. Jerome has shifted, in his discussion of virginal and chaste pagans, from exposition to attack; the enemy is sexual woman. His own appended comments reveal his concern: "I know that I have said much more in this catalogue of women than custom allows . . . but what should I do, when the women of our time quote 'authority' to me, and before the first husband is buried, repeat from memory the precepts allowing a second marriage?" (Jerome, *Adversus Jovinianum*, cols. 288–289). Jerome is trying to shame the Christian women of his own day by using unflattering comparisons to pagan women who remained chaste.

With this specific statement in mind, we may sense an incongruity when reexamining his list of virtuous pagan women. Chastity in women was valued in classical times, as in most times and cultures, because it assured bloodlines and continuation of property. But virgins in pagan antiquity wielded certain powers far exceeding those of chaste wives. Some of Jerome's virgins engage in masculine activities such as hunting and fighting; he mentions Atalanta and Camilla, among others. Some gained wisdom and prophecy, like the Sybils, "ten whose sign was virginity, and prophecy the reward of virginity" (Jerome, col. 283). Others, including Cassandra, Chryseis, and innumerable priestesses of Diana and Vesta, performed special religious and civic functions. So it appears that virgins, when honored by the ancients, gained freedoms and privileges not usually given to women. The lack of equivalent honor given to virgin men may suggest that abstinence from the natural functions of one's own sex gave one the qualities of the other sex. Thus, these virgin women performed "manly" roles, while classical writers seem to have considered virgin men effeminate.

For Jerome, though he uses classical examples, the division falls along different lines. Although Jerome honors chaste women by calling them "manly,"[36] he would not have approved of women warriors— much less women priests!—in his own day. For him, men are spirit and women flesh; any carnal desire a man feels for a woman pulls him down to her level. Paradoxically, in classical terms, Jerome and other Christian writers see a man's desire for a woman as making him effeminate. One becomes more "manly" the more one avoids the female sex. By using these examples of pagan virgins and their exploits, however, Jerome hands down to later writers the classical view of these women as admirable figures. He also confirms the lessons that could be drawn from the *Heroides* and the sorrowing fields: women can enjoy greater independence and freedom when they remain strangers to men and to passion. Acting "like a woman"—that is, responding to the demands of the flesh—incapacitates women in every other realm of life.

Some antifeminists claim that her sexual and procreative functions are a woman's only virtue. As I have mentioned, Jerome feels that abstinence from these functions is a woman's only virtue: "The consulship ennobles men; eloquence raises an eternal name; military glory and a triumph immortalize a new clan. . . . [But] the virtue of a woman is exclusively chastity" (Jerome, *Adversus Jovinianum*, col. 294). Jerome believes that chastity is a special virtue in women, not because men should not be chaste, but because women possess no other virtue worthy of note. Those pagan women who followed the hunt or acted as priestesses and prophetesses are all very well as examples of virginity, but he would not have wished to encourage such masculine activities among contemporary women.

THE FOURTEENTH CENTURY

Ovid, Vergil, and, to a lesser extent, Saint Jerome are named by Chaucer and recognized by critics as among the sources of *The*

Legend of Good Women. By Chaucer's day, the catalogue of women had attained tremendous popularity both as a literary device to enrich a longer work and as an independent genre. Among medieval catalogues by Chaucer's near-contemporaries, two stand out as especially important. They are Boccaccio's *De Claris Mulieribus* and Christine de Pizan's *Livre de la Cité des Dames* (*Book of the City of Ladies*). Boccaccio's work, composed around 1360, was known and used by Chaucer;[37] Christine's was written around 1407, after Chaucer's death. Although she appears not to have made use of the *Legend,* I feel that the *Cité* deserves consideration here. It deals directly with the anti-feminism implicit in most catalogues that claim to praise women. In so doing, it dispels the notion that medieval people shared a set of beliefs that they were incapable of examining critically—or of ridiculing. Christine's work differs greatly from Chaucer's in tone and purpose, yet there are significant underlying connections between the two works.

Most fourteenth-century catalogues of good women follow Jerome's precedent by using classical heroines. Female saints, especially virgin martyrs, enjoyed great popularity in a separate tradition; they rarely appear alongside pagans in the catalogues. Many factors could account for this separation. Different sources provide their stories. The popularity of classical literature in the fourteenth century may have led authors to treat this "new" subject matter with special favor. The pagans' remoteness in time and tradition also allowed a wider range of action for female characters and a greater freedom in dealing with sexual mores.

Boccaccio explains his own choice in the preface to *De Claris Mulieribus.* He will not deal with Christian saints, he says, because their stories have already been told. He also distinguishes between Christian and Hebrew women, who attained greatness by following commandments laid down for them, and the pagans, who act "through some natural gift or instinct, or rather spurred by desire for this fleeting glory."[38] Boccaccio also includes the stories of historical and contemporary women, often pointing up the contrast between their vices and the virtues of pagan women.

Fourteenth-century authors delighted in the heroines from classical literature and mythology and used them to prove all sorts of things about women. They imposed various moral frameworks that were common to the rhetorical technique of the medieval catalogue upon the stories of Ovid, Vergil, and others. When Dido and Medea appear in the lists, they are labeled as "good" or "bad" women rather than being treated as human beings with complex motives for their actions. Their complexity is played down so that they may fit the lesson they are to prove.

BOCCACCIO

Boccaccio's *De Claris Mulieribus*, a collection of short biographies of women, represents the culmination of his portrayals of women in romances, fabliaux, and satires. Critics disagree as to whether *DCM* offers genuine praise of women. Some say that it does, others that it tries and fails; some believe that its elevation of a few women at the expense of all the rest reveals fundamental misogyny.[39] Boccaccio's moral pronouncements about women's conduct often cross the line into invective, and even his words of praise include much satire.

This confusion results in part from his belief that women are naturally inferior to men. With this conviction, he finds the most to praise in women who transcend their sex. He sees these women as taking on "masculine" characteristics such as moral and physical strength and courage. "If men should be praised whenever they perform great deeds (with the strength which Nature has given them), how much more should women be extolled (almost all of whom are endowed with tenderness, frail bodies, and sluggish minds by Nature), if they have acquired a manly spirit and if with keen intelligence and remarkable fortitude they have dared undertake and have accomplished even the most difficult deeds?" (p. xxxvii).

The problem implicit here does not remain hidden for long. It does not matter greatly if women are naturally lustful and treacherous, if they are also naturally weak and cowardly. But when certain natural limitations are transcended, others may be also—with less desirable effects. When Boccaccio praises manly qualities, therefore, he does so in virgins or chaste matrons; and in most cases, he praises the exercise of their manly virtues on behalf of men. The boldness of Hypsicratea, who dressed as a man to follow her husband into battle, receives commendation. But the same boldness can turn an unregenerate woman into a monster. Boccaccio's most vehement passages condemn women like Clytemnestra, of whom he says: "I do not know which I condemn more, the crime or the daring. The first was a great evil which that noble man had not deserved; the second was the more abominable as it was the more unbecoming to the perfidious woman" (p. 72). Throughout *DCM,* Boccaccio tries to give moral instruction to a sex whose "natural" state he despises but whose unnatural state he finds threatening. *DCM* includes seven of the ten women who appear in Chaucer's *Legend.* In most cases Boccaccio treats them predictably according to the stories. He finds pathetic the story of Thisbe, who died a virgin, but notes that she "became famous among men for the tragic end of her love, rather than for any accomplishments" (p. 25). Hypermnestra and Hypsipyle show the right kinds of devotion, the first to her husband, the second to her father. Lucretia "cleansed her shame harshly, and for this reason she should be exalted with worthy praise for her chastity, which can never be sufficiently lauded" (p. 103). In praising her for committing suicide after she was raped (and in suggesting that the "shame" of her rape needed cleansing), Boccaccio goes against no lesser authority than Saint Augustine; but this exaltation of Lucretia was fairly common. Cleopatra and Medea call forth diatribes against lust and greed. The acts of incest and murder committed by Cleopatra, the murder and infanticide done by Medea, are chronicled in detail to show the extent of their depravity.

In telling Dido's story, Boccaccio passes over the familiar accounts by Ovid and Vergil to use a less familiar version by Justinus. This biographical sketch again illustrates the paramount importance of chastity in Boccaccio's valuation of women. He begins by stating that the accusations against Dido are false: "I should like to speak somewhat more at length in her praise, if with my modest remarks I may, perhaps, partly remove the infamy undeservedly cast on her widowhood" (p. 86).

He explains that her people tricked her into giving up her vow in order to protect them by marrying a neighboring king. Dido pretended to go along; she built a bonfire, ostensibly to placate the spirit of her dead husband, then threw herself into it. In this version, Aeneas' arrival was coincidental to her suicide for chastity's sake. Boccaccio waxes eloquent: "O inviolate honor of chastity! O venerable and eternal example of constant widowhood." He quickly turns the story of Dido's suicide into a harangue against widows who wish to remarry, sounding very much like Jerome in his condemnation of Christian women who fall short of pagan examples.

Boccaccio's defense of Dido's chastity against those usually considered the "authorities" shows the extent to which they could contradict

FIGURE 2. Medea. By permission of Bodleian Library, Oxford.

each other. Conflicting versions existed of the stories of Dido, Helen, and many others. Yet, an author could not simply add or omit anything he wanted in retelling old stories, since the more familiar versions would certainly be remembered. In the case of Dido, Boccaccio deliberately challenged Vergil's treatment of her, marshaling his evidence to show that she had been maligned. Here and elsewhere in *DCM*, he took the familiar versions of the stories into account, attempting to determine the more reliable sources and the versions to be taken more seriously. His choices often seem haphazard, though, and influenced by personal preference. Above all, his desire to fit all women into classifications of "good" and "bad" undermines the pretense of objectivity.

Boccaccio's *De Claris Mulieribus* and other catalogues of women provided Chaucer with raw material. They also provided him with examples of the tortuous reasoning often employed by those who undertook to define women's virtue by example. Chaucer knows and plays upon this aspect of the stories: that they can prove any point an author wants to make—that they take the shape of the mold into which they are poured. Yet Boccaccio's treatment of Dido shows that authors expected these stories to be known and that departures from well-known sources would have been noted. Boccaccio also provides another useful lesson for Chaucer: that the catalogues reveal more about their authors than they do about their supposed subjects. Chaucer may have adapted Boccaccio's unwitting self-revelation in creating the narrator of his *Legend*. Boccaccio employs rhetoric to praise or denounce women according to whether they fit his definition of virtue; Chaucer's narrator takes a definition of virtue (given to him by the God of Love) and uses rhetoric to make a diverse group of women fit it.

CHRISTINE DE PIZAN

De Claris Mulieribus began to be used by French writers soon after its completion around 1360; the first French translation appeared around 1400. Christine de Pizan wrote her encyclopedic *Cité des Dames* when the popularity of *DCM* was at its peak, and she relied on it heavily. Christine accepts traditional roles for women, and she echoes the belief that chastity is woman's greatest virtue.[40] She differs from Boccaccio, however, in two important ways. First, she does not despise women's supposed natural qualities or their traditional occupations.[41] She views their roles as different from those of men, but as no less necessary in God's plan. Second, she sees women who are unchaste or evil as pitiable human beings who have made wrong choices. They are not to her, as they are to Boccaccio, horrifying examples of the degradation to which all women threaten to slip.

Most importantly for our purposes, Christine offers a different perspective on women who destroy themselves for love. Christine wrote the *Cité* only a few years after Chaucer's death, and it enjoyed immediate success. This fact suggests that at least some medieval readers were already capable of hearing her message about these women—that this kind of "martyrdom" is not admirable but foolish and wrong.

Following the dictates of fashion, Christine offers Dido, Medea, Thisbe, Hero, and others as examples of women's fidelity in love. She makes quite clear, however, that while such "foolish love" (p. 202) may argue for women's constancy in general, the constancy of these women is misdirected. Dido "loved too much" (p. 189), Medea "loved . . . with a too great and too constant love" (p. 189), Thisbe and Pyramus were "overwhelmed by too much love" (p. 191). She concludes her stories of love's martyrs by saying, "these pitiful examples . . . should in no way move women's hearts to set themselves adrift in the dangerous and damnable sea of foolish love, for its end is always detrimental and harmful to their bodies, their property, their honor, and—most important of all—their souls. Women . . . should . . . not listen to those who incessantly strive to deceive them in such cases" (p. 202). Although Christine, like Jerome and Boccaccio, exhorts women to be chaste, her reasons run counter to theirs. She sees "women's nature"— their passion, their sex—not as loathsome powers to be thwarted but as treasures to be protected. She also knows that "defenses" of women who destroy themselves for men promote misogyny just as forcefully as do straightforward works of antifeminism.

THE LEGEND OF GOOD WOMEN

The *Legend of Good Women* offers many clues as to how it should be read—too many, for they are contradictory, even deliberately misleading. The "voice" of the poet is unusually direct, didactic, and— even for a Chaucerian narrator—untrustworthy. I shall argue that the *Legend* is the supreme example of its genre and a devastating parody of that genre: the catalogue of good women to end all catalogues of good women.[42]

The *Legend* claims to praise women who were faithful lovers and to show them as representing the majority of their sex. The undercutting that many see at work questions this purpose but makes possible others. Some have less to do with women, the "subject," than with works of literature and the act of writing. The *Legend* mocks the catalogues' attempts to define an abstract ideal by concrete examples that repeatedly fail to fit. In exposing the catalogues' failure to reduce mythological characters (much less real women) to formulae, Chaucer questions all the authorities who compose such catalogues or supply the material. Just as he does in his early works and in many of the *Canterbury Tales,* Chaucer here creates a storyteller who in the course of talking about something else reveals much more about himself. He had models in Boccaccio and Jerome, particularly—men whose writing about women attempts to express objective truth but actually shows us much more about their hopes, fears, and intense subjective involvement in regard to their subject.[43]

Nevertheless, the *Legend* does have significant things to say about women. Although its characters are not really women, but men's literary portayals of women, they carry the same "psychological realism" that readers have found in Ovid's *Heroides*. That is, they represent quite accurately what some men and women think women really are like. Several thousand years of showing women as victims of their own passion cannot fail to have an effect upon how we perceive women in life—and thus, upon what women are.

Seeing the women of the *Legend* as victims of the ideal of chaste love does not absolve them of responsibility for their fate. Finally, all the women accept the ideal and judge themselves by it. By accepting what men define as female virtue, Chaucer's "good woman" attains her only available moral stature—and her only superiority to men. Being an innocent victim gives her a sort of moral purity that can seem to make any suffering worthwhile.

Chaucer's *Legend* shows this belief about women as firmly in control of his heroines, and of the literary genre in which the God of Love forces him to write. In the *Legend*, women can do anything, good or evil, with their lives, or nothing at all, and receive exactly the same hyperbolic praise—provided that they destroy themselves for the ideal of chaste love. After their deaths, they are rewarded with eternal contemplation of their superiority to the men for whom they sacrificed themselves.

THE PROLOGUE TO THE LEGEND

The prologue[44] to the *Legend* builds on the situation at the ending of *Troilus and Criseyde*. In the course of trying to end that poem, the narrator turns abruptly to address the women in his audience: "Beseeching every lady bright of hue, and every gentlewoman, of whatever rank, that although Criseyde was untrue, she not be angry with me on account of that guilt. You may read about her guilty deeds in other books; and I would more gladly write, if you like, about Penelope's faithfulness and good Alceste. Nor do I say this only for men, but mostly for women who have been betrayed by false folk; God give them sorrow, amen! who with their great wit and subtlety betray you. And this moves me to speak, and in effect I pray you all, beware of men, and listen to what I say!" (pp. 478–79). Chaucer's words at the end of *Troilus* begin the characterization of the *Legend*'s narrator, whose stated purposes are to write of good women and to warn them against men. Chaucer's desire to write a comedy inspires him to create this narrator, who is laughable in many ways—not the least in the methods he chooses to praise women and blame men. This narrator will go to any lengths to avoid repeating his thankless task, in *Troilus*, of writing about a guilty woman. In his eagerness henceforth to write good things about women, he is willing to forfeit any other goal, including adherence to those authorities who are urged upon him as sources—Ovid, Jerome, and the other "clerks."

The narrator's address to women at the end of *Troilus* foreshadows something of the *Legend*'s tone as well. It is darkly humorous, in a way, to imagine an audience whose chief reaction to *Troilus and Criseyde* is indignation at the author's choice of an unfaithful heroine. Likewise, one must laugh a bit at the narrator himself, whose grief at his heroine's treachery forces him to deny his sense of her complexity, to make of her another example of fickle womanhood. Yet comedy complements tragedy here, while in the *Legend* comedy predominates. As a test of their relative tones, imagine Chaucer promising at the end of his tragic masterpiece *Troilus* to write about Thisbe's faithfulness and good Medea.

We can only guess at Chaucer's true motives in writing the *Legend*.[45] Perhaps women of the court really did object to *Troilus* as antifeminist. Perhaps the popularity of the genre induced him to write a long catalogue of his own. I believe that Chaucer may indeed have been angered at criticism of *Troilus* as antifeminist. People may have asked, as he says at the end of *Troilus* that they did, "Why not write in praise of women? Why not write about good women like Alceste?" He then may have taken this "good advice" to extremes in order to reveal it for what it is—antifeminism in a much more insidious form than *Troilus* could ever be. *Troilus* tells the story of a charming woman, the personification of ideal human love, who turns out to be less perfect than she seems. The *Legend*'s heroines are throughout exactly what they seem at first—virtuous to a fault. They also represent the horrors that can result from imposing a single standard for virtue on half of humanity—one from which the other half is effectively exempt.

Whatever Chaucer's reasons for writing the *Legend*, the accusations of having defamed women that are leveled at him in its prologue serve an important purpose. They continue this fictional narrator's fictionally heightened dilemma.[46] Cupid and Alceste accuse the narrator of defaming women and romantic love. Their accusations and the penalty they exact force the narrator to praise women beyond the bounds of reason and, in some cases, against the evidence of the very sources they have told him to use. Through this narrator, Chaucer exposes the lack of reasoning shown by almost all the catalogues of good women. These catalogues glorify qualities in excess: not just courage, but the ability to lead an army in battle and decapitate an enemy; not just strong-mindedness, but monomania; not just faithful love, but martyrdom for a wholly unworthy man.

The exaltation of the heroines by degrading their lovers and men in general reveals other aspects of these catalogues. Even though they seem to be illustrating some truth about human nature, they leave human complexity and individuality totally out of account. One effect of Chaucer's blaming men for every conceivable ill may have been to show them how women feel when they hear themselves so treated. But most importantly, the exaggeration is simply allowed to swell until it collapses under its own weight. When we realize that we cannot take seriously a tenth of what Chaucer is saying about men, we find we must question all the claims of the poem about men, women, virtue, love, old books, authority—and about its own purpose.

Chaucer gives great importance in the *Legend* to the problematic relationship between experience and authority—so much that he devotes the first twenty-eight lines of the prologue to it. Critics disagree as to whether this passage is a serious statement of belief in authority (with religious overtones) or an elaborate joke. I see it, primarily at least, as the latter. Chaucer's actual treatment of authority in the poem ranges from statements of slavish adherence to questions about authorial reliability, even to unacknowledged omissions, additions, and distortions. The lines themselves, moreover, resemble the clearly humorous opening lines of *The House of Fame*. That poem's narrator mentions seemingly every possible type of dream and every conceivable explanation of their significance. Just when the reader expects him to make clear his important new contribution to dream lore, the narrator ends by saying that dreams have an important function but that he himself does not know what it is. Similarly, the lines from the *Legend* contain an amusingly anticlimactic proverb—"even Bernard the Monk did not see all!"—and conclusion—"To old books we must give the credit due; / Where we've no other proof, let's think them true."

To what does this last injunction apply? One answer, in terms of the poem, must be—to the existence of good women. E. Talbot Donaldson says of these lines, "Old books describe faithful women and [the narrator] is perfectly willing to believe old books, but personally he has never met a faithful woman."[47] The narrator, so eager to defend women, would never say such a thing outright. The lines, with their tortuous wording and apparent contradictions, say it in spite of his intent.

Perversely enough—and this is the problem in *Troilus*—old books also describe unfaithful women and women who, if indeed faithful to their lovers, are not good in any other sense of the word. It is these authorities whom the narrator must combat, holding up the standard of praise for women against an onslaught of offending details. Like any good propagandist, he finds the proof of his information in the extent to which it supports his views. "Experience"—what one learns from life and the evidence of one's senses—dwindles, in the stories themselves, to warnings that men are still betraying women and that women ought to beware. The opening lines, seen in this light, have another meaning. They cast doubt over both what one sees and what one reads, and over the judgments—good or bad, heaven or hell—that one draws from both kinds of proof. The martyrs of love are in Cupid's Paradise, but they, like the inhabitants of Vergil's sorrowing fields, are women "whom harsh love destroyed with cruel ruin."

The narrator's lack of experience with real women and his unsuitability as a lover are emphasized by the diversion of his romantic affections to books and daisies. Descriptions of the typical lover's sleeplessness and worship of his lady are applied to this fictional poet, who loves daisies and old books the way most men love women. The narrator as a lover of books and of women from books appears in Chaucer's early poems. The devotion turned toward daisies, however, has not appeared before in his works. Some critics suggest a topical reference to the courtly love debates between supporters of the flower and those of the leaf (*Legend,* p. 480). Not enough details survive to give us any clear idea of what Chaucer might have meant by referring to this debate. In any case, he specifically disclaims preference for either side, flower or leaf (lines 188–196), and states that his poem has to do with events of an earlier time. What must be important are the daisy's eventual identification as the emblem of Alceste and the poet-narrator's exaggerated devotion to both the lady and the flower.

This devotion, derived from the French *marguerite* (daisy) poems,[48] seems harmless enough. Again, though, Chaucer has apparently taken a literary device (here, the flower worshiped as lady) and brought it into comic juxtaposition with real life. As it turns out, love is never a safe emotion, even when directed toward such an apparently benign object as a flower. The narrator will be as browbeaten by a daisy turned imperious woman as any fictional lover was ever tormented by his exacting mistress.

The beautiful May morning in which the narrator gives free rein to his worship of the daisy also delights the small birds. In this passage (lines 130–170), we see love governing unruly nature according to its precepts. With the "unkind" birds (the word in Middle English connotes unnaturalness), a false note jars the harmony. "Unnatural" behavior has entered the natural world. Paradoxically, this supposedly unnatural behavior is in reality most natural. Not all birds mate for life, and in the Middle Ages some were emblems of fickleness and lust. In avian terms, their "unkindness" occurs as a matter of course, but here it is treated as something to be repented. When penitent birds swear "on the blossoms" to be true, we feel that the vow counts for little. The birds' renewed fidelity will surely follow its natural course, the ephemeral course of blossoms. But that is as it should be; nature did not design all birds to be faithful.

The unsettling effect of this passage arises from obvious parallels between these birds and the men and women of the legends. It prefigures, on several levels, the paradigmatic situation of men betraying women. The fowlers who trap small birds with "sophistry" (usually thought of as verbal cunning), as well as the unkind birds who swear to be true, call to mind those false and flattering men—Aeneas, Jason, and the rest. Their victims, whose initial "reluctance" is tempered by "pity" so that "mercy" overcomes "right," strongly resemble Cupid's martyrs, the women destroyed by love. In the legends, Chaucer often points to women's pity and mercy as awakening their passion and clouding their judgment. Here, the narrator awkwardly insists on the virtue of the birds' forgiving their false lovers. The obtrusive denial of foolishness only makes one wonder whether their supposedly virtuous pity is really such a good idea.

Most readers find this passage conventionally, even touchingly, romantic; yet Chaucer provides one more warning against a too-easy acceptance of it. He frames these lines describing small birds with two Ovidian references to rapes. Europa, "the daughter of Agenor," was abducted by Zeus in the guise of a bull.[49] Chloris became known as

Flora after her rape by Zephyr.[50] Thinly veiled warnings of violence and deceit in this passage prefigure the *Legend* as a whole as well as the individual legends. The ideals of love war with the demands of lust; nature and society are out of harmony, mutually destructive. Idealism fares little better than cynical self-indulgence; there are hints of self-deception and moral coercion in the "innocent" birds who extract promises of a faithfulness that runs contrary to their lovers' nature and that they have good reason to doubt.

Returning from the field where he has seen the daisy and witnessed the birds, the narrator falls asleep. He dreams that he is again kneeling by the daisy when he sees in the distance the God of Love, hand-in-hand with a "queen" dressed in green, white, and gold and followed by a retinue of women. Cupid, catching sight of the narrator at his vigil beside the daisy, approaches with his entourage. He accuses the narrator of having no right to be near the flower and goes on to charge him with libeling love's servants and treating the service of love as "folly." Cupid claims irrefutable proof: has not the poet translated *The Romance of the Rose*, which discourages "wise folk" from loving? Has he not written "as he pleased" of Criseyde (an ironic accusation in light of that poem's narrator)? The God of Love's admonition (G-version) contains a passage placing the collection of stories to follow firmly within the tradition of catalogues of women:

> Was there no worthy subject in your mind,
> Or in your books could you have failed to find
> For me some tale of women good and true?
> Yes, God knows, sixty books—some old, some new—
> You have yourself, with stories worth attention
> In which both Greeks and Romans have made mention
> Of sundry women, and the lives they had,
> Always a hundred good against one bad.
> God knows this fact, and so do all the clerks,
> Who are accustomed to peruse such works.
> What say Valerius, Titus, Claudian?
> What says Jerome against Jovinian?
> How chaste are maidens, and how true are wives,
> How steadfast widows are through all their lives—
> This Jerome tells, nor are their numbers small—
> At least a hundred there must be in all [lines 270–285].

As we have seen, and as knowledgeable contemporary readers would have realized, Cupid is here presenting a distorted picture of what Jerome and others wrote about women. Clearly, the God of Love is one of those defenders of women who bends his sources to suit his arguments. This passage alerts the reader to expect other instances of distortion in the poem.

The God of Love goes on to describe what all these clerks say about women; we see again the ideal of chastity as the only criterion for virtue in women and the choice of pagan women to prove the point. These women were so true in love, he says, that rather than take a new lover they chose to die by various means; he mentions burning, throat-slitting, and drowning. And they kept their maiden, married, or widowed state "not to emulate the saints, / But to be virtuous and free from taints, / And so that men should find in them no flaw" (lines 296–298). This distinction recalls one of Boccaccio's explanations of why he chose to write about pagan women. The passage announces Chaucer's intention of following the pattern set by Jerome and Boccaccio. If he wants to ridicule the catalogues' excesses, the choice is well made. The distinction that Cupid makes between Christian women martyred for "holiness" and pagan women martyred for "virtue" also cuts off the women of the *Legend* from Christian goals and rewards. What these women suffer or die for is sexual love (though not exactly as the God of Love describes it) and reputation.

When Alceste steps in to defend the poet against Cupid's accusations, she suggests the penance of writing about women who were true lovers all their lives, in order to help the cause of Cupid as much as he had hindered it by earlier works. Cupid agrees, and the poet then receives Alceste's further explanation of his sentence (lines 481–511). Cupid, at the end of the prologue, suggests that the poet begin with the ladies of the *balade* (lines 654–658). Leaving out Absalom and Jonathan, they are Esther, Penelope, Marcia the wife of Cato, Iseult, Helen, Lavinia, Lucrece, Polyxena, Cleopatra, Thisbe, Hero, Dido, Laodamia, Phyllis, Canace, Hypsipyle, Hypermnestra, and Ariadne. Chaucer is supposed to tell the highlights of their life stories. Even the list proposed by Cupid himself conforms only sporadically to the ideal of chaste devotion that he has endorsed. Some of these women are known for acts of incest, infidelity, deceit, and murder.

Faithfulness in love, from Ovid, not chastity, from Jerome, acts as the overriding requirement here. Jerome's women are true to their virginity or chastity; those in the *Legend* are mostly true to their lovers outside of marriage. John Fyler sees conflict resulting from the imposition of a Christian frame upon pagan, Ovidian content. Thus, "problems arise when Chaucer tries to flesh out this catalogue with the hyperbole of saints' lives." [51] Certainly this unlikely juxtaposition furthers Chaucer's comic purpose and his serious theme. Nevertheless, the difference between these women may not be as radical as it appears. Jerome's martyrs die or take other measures, lest they violate their chaste or virginal honor. Ovid's martyrs also stake everything on their virginity or chastity; they trade these most valuable commodities for promises of faithful love and marriage. When they are deserted or betrayed, they react much as Jerome's martyrs do. Both groups sacrifice themselves to the same ideal: a woman should undergo suffering or death rather than live unchastely.

Jerome's women sacrifice themselves to avoid falling. Ovid's sacrifice themselves, usually, as a result of having fallen and then having lost the men for whom they fell. Chaucer includes some of both among his martyrs. He keeps constant, however, the idea of reputation, "name," as the motive behind all their actions. Whether a woman's fate results from having kept her name or from having not kept it seems to matter not at all. The stories, and the rhetoric of praise, treat them as different reenactments of the same archetypal pattern. Although the women of the *Legend* claim to have suffered martyrdom for the sake of their lovers, the individual men have little importance in comparison to the overriding idea of reputation. Even Alceste and Hypermnestra, the most unselfish and efficacious of the martyrs, die for their "wifehood" more than for their husbands.

Alceste's story does not appear among the legends, but her importance in the prologue demands attention. Unnamed at first, she is the God of Love's "queen" and intercedes with him on behalf of the narrator, though the arguments she uses are hardly flattering (see lines 412–416 for examples).[52] Near the end of the prologue, Cupid reveals that this lady is Alceste, who gave herself to death in place of her husband. The use of her story raises two main questions. Why has Chaucer invented the story of her metamorphosis into a daisy, and what kind of "paradise" does she now inhabit?

On the evidence of the poem, we know that the daisy ("day's eye") opens to the sun and closes at evening, loves light and hates darkness. This image of a flower responding to the motions of the sun recalls

Ovid's story of Clytie, who, turned into a sunflower, followed her lover Apollo with her "eyes" forever after.[53] The story could thus represent exaggerated female devotion to love and the lover. As an image of devotion the daisy is precisely appropriate, but who or what is the "sun" that Alceste worships? Her husband Admetus' name is not even mentioned in the *Legend,* and only the slightest mention is made of him as the occasion for her sacrifice. It is clearly the sacrifice itself, not the supposed object, that is important. At one point in the prologue, the ladies in Cupid's entourage surround the daisy and address it as the worthiest of their number.[54] Alceste, as the daisy and as a woman, is at once the object of worship and a worshiper. It is difficult to escape the conclusion that she is worshiping herself, and that the ladies are worshiping, in her emblem, their own acts.

Alceste, Cupid says, "of noble love . . . taught the excellence, / Especially of wifely innocence, / And all the boundaries a wife should keep." This passage makes her self-sacrifice the pattern for those of Cleopatra, Medea, and the other martyrs. The Paradise in which the poem places her is Cupid's court. She appears hand-in-hand with the god himself, followed by a group of nineteen ladies in regal clothing. These are apparently the women whose stories Chaucer planned to include. After them comes a numberless throng of women, all of whom were true in love. All these women supposedly suffered or died for their lovers, but they are not reunited with them in Paradise. Echoes of Vergil's sorrowing fields suggest that it was their own passion and "name," not their loved ones, for which these women suffered. Since the legends repeatedly dwell on men's unworthiness (as Alceste herself does, lines 486–489),[55] their absence seems to be, at best, a matter of indifference to the ladies. It may even constitute part of their reward. In any case, it prefigures the legends' emphasis on the women's virtue and their lovers' viciousness and makes even more dubious the motives for, and the value of, their self-sacrifice.

We do not know where Chaucer got his version of Alceste's story.[56] It would seem to be the perfect example of self-sacrificing love, but even the earliest accounts reflect conflicting beliefs about her motives. Chaucer refers to Plato's *Symposium,* which he calls *Agathon* after one of its characters, as having told her story; he might have known the work, or parts of it, from some intermediary. In fact, the *Symposium* refers to Alceste twice. The first time she is admired as a lover, though judged inferior to Achilles in his love for Patroclus.[57] Later Diotima, a prophetess, reflects on this judgment: "Do you imagine that Alcestis would have died to save Admetus, or Achilles to avenge Patroclus . . . if they had not imagined that the memory of their virtues, which still survives among us, would be immortal?"[58] For Diotima, this drive toward immortality is valued source of virtue. In context of the *Legend*, this passage reinforces the idea that Alceste died not for her husband, but for her name as a wife.

Euripides, a playwright very aware of the mixed motives and conflicting points of view always present in human activity, depicts Alceste as conscious of her moral superiority and eager to exploit it. At the point of death, she makes Admetus promise never to marry again, calling this "recompense . . . not enough, oh, never enough, since nothing is enough to make up for a life."[59]

Chaucer may not have been aware of these passages from the classics. Yet the recurrence of undercutting in these accounts of Alceste makes us wonder if something in the human intellect may *have* to question such extreme generosity. Even in classical accounts, Alceste's moral superiority is somewhat suspect; in Christian terms, it is obviously inferior to the sacrifices of holy martyrs—and of Christ himself.[60] In patterning his *Legend* after the stories of saints, however humorously, Chaucer invites comparison between Alceste's and the other good women's self-sacrifice and the sacrifice at the heart of the Christian religion. This parallel only further diminishes the women, however, since they are worshiping their own virtue rather than any ideal beyond it, and their objects are clearly unworthy. Following the analogy between the *Legend* and saints' lives, the men of the *Legend* occupy the position both of god (the ideal for which a martyr sacrifices herself) and of Roman emperor (the tormenter responsible for the martyrdom). If the *Legend* expresses the significance of Christian martyrdom, it does so by making the contrast in motives and rewards so evident.

The purpose of the prologue becomes clearer in light of the tales themselves. In them Chaucer carries out the commands given by the God of Love and Alceste as well as he can. Since the commands contradict each other—"write only good things about women, and start with Cleopatra"—the legends must be understood as much in terms of what they avoid saying as of what they say. From avoidance, enhanced with rhetoric, comes the humor and meaning of the legends.

THE LEGENDS

In the individual legends, Chaucer makes all his heroines, with their very different stories, conform to an unvarying pattern of victimization. To a quite remarkable degree, the legends succeed in making the heroines interchangeable with one another. This uniformity—so different from the *Canterbury Tales*—often makes readers impatient with the legends. Some see the *Legend* as a failure because of it; others look that much more carefully for any differences on which to focus among the stories.[61] The evidence suggests, however, that in this work Chaucer means to create uniformity from the raw material of diversity. The prologue dramatizes this purpose in the fiction of the poet whom Cupid calls back to orthodoxy. The comedy and the theme of the *Legend* come from this dilemma of a poet coerced into making a highly disparate group of women conform to the narrow ideals set forth by the God of Love—forced to become, like the women he writes about, a martyr to the ideal of chaste love.

Eleanor Winsor Leach points out that Chaucer relies mainly on three aspects of the catalogue device in his legends: amplification, abbreviation, and reference to authority.[62] These three rhetorical techniques, common to most catalogues, are exaggerated. He amplifies the goodness of women and the deceitful nature of men, abbreviates the stories to conceal evidence to the contrary, and cites authority most slavishly where he flouts it most boldly. In order to prove his thesis about women's virtue, he must employ this distortion. Yet, as Leach has shown, Chaucer undermines his thesis again and again. Ironic discrepancies between what his sources say and what appears in Chaucer's rhetorically altered versions form much of the *Legend*'s humor.

Leach has observed that when Chaucer leaves out a detail damaging to one of his heroines, he usually reminds the reader that he has done so, defeating his supposed purpose of whitewashing. He claims various pretexts for leaving something out: he is doing so, he says, to save time or to avoid dwelling on painful subjects. Of this practice of abbreviation, Leach says, "'we may observe that in the legends dealing with incontrovertibly 'good' women, Thisbe and Lucretia, Chaucer does not call our attention to any expurgations, a fact which bears witness to the consciousness of his practice elsewhere. The opening legend, that of Cleopatra . . . contains three striking abridgements. The opening lines . . . are economical. . . . Behind this vague opening lie such events as Cleopatra's murder of her brother and the affair with Julius Caesar which establishes the queen on her throne" (Leach, p. 65).

The two other abridgements are his omission of details of the wedding feast (which may not have happened; Leach, p. 107) as "too long to tell"; and of her grief at her and Antony's defeat (when she attempted to seduce Octavian; Leach, pp. 66, 109) as "too sad to tell." Beverly Taylor's article on "the medieval Cleopatra" also supplies abundant details testifying to the reputation of Cleopatra—details that Chaucer tellingly omits. Taylor argues that, in view of Chaucer's sources, placement of the notorious Egyptian queen as first among the heroines establishes his ironic intent.[63]

Ironic omissions are also plentiful in the stories from classical sources. Dido's often-mentioned vow of chaste widowhood disappears. This omission might seem to benefit her reputation; yet Chaucer does not fail to remind us that she was once the wife of Sychaeus (lines 1004–1005). Hypsipyle is "the daughter of Thoas, the former king" (line 1467), our only reminder that the women of Lemnos had killed all their men. Hypsipyle herself spared her father's life, but to praise her for that would be to condemn all the other women on the island.[64] Similarly, the fifty sons of Aegyptus and fifty daughters of Danaus disappear after the first mention. He does not reveal that all fifty daughters except Hypsipyle obeyed their father—married their cousins and killed them on their wedding night. To reveal this fact would be to go against the proportions—a hundred good women for every bad—established by Cupid. Again, however, he keeps the omitted material in view; as Fyler says, "Chaucer lets slip enough to make a hash of the story as he tells it: the cruel father wonders which one of his nephews will kill him . . . but orders only Hypermnestra to become a murderess" (Fyler, p. 102). Chaucer consistently omits incidents in which the good women take violent revenge on the men who caused their suffering. Medea killed her two children by Jason to avenge his betrayal of her; but this fact, like the text of her letter to Jason, is for Chaucer "too long for me to write" (line 1679). Again, however, he makes sure that we do not forget the censored material. He has Hypsipyle, the heroine whom Jason seduced and abandoned before he met Medea, curse her rival, praying

> that, before too long a while,
> She who from her had taken Jason's heart

Would find herself cast in the victim's part
And that her childen she would have to kill,
And all of them that let him do his will.[65]

Procne killed her son by Tereus and served his flesh to his father in revenge for the rape and mutilation of her sister Philomela. Chaucer passes over this incident, blandly stating that

The remnant is not burdensome to tell,
For this is all of it: thus was she served
Who'd done no evil and had not deserved,
That she knew of, harm from this cruel man.[66]

Here Chaucer slips in the troublesome phrase "that she knew of," casting doubt on his protestations of Philomela's innocence. When readers begin to wonder how Philomela could have deserved her fate, they may find themselves forced to reread her story with more suspicious eyes.

The legends are rife with this kind of troublesome phrasing, presented in such abbreviated form that we are left to question every assertion made by the beleagered narrator. Another example appears in the legend of Ariadne. That heroine arranges a betrothal between her sister and an otherwise unidentified "son" of Theseus. Theseus himself is only twenty-three at the time and claims to have loved Ariadne faithfully, sight unseen, for seven years. The mention of a son presumably old enough to marry Phaedra, who is apparently close in age to Ariadne, defies logical explanation. It may point to a future time, long after the final incident of Chaucer's legend, in which Theseus abandons Ariadne for her sister. Later events of the story have Phaedra falling in love with Theseus' son Hippolytus and bringing disaster upon them all. (According to the myth, Theseus is actually much older than Phaedra; Hippolytus is his son by Hippolyta, who predates both Ariadne and Phaedra as his wife.) Recalling these details, we may question whether any of the characters deserve our sympathy. Such details appear insignificant, if puzzling, on the surface but are capable of changing the effect of an entire legend by calling attention to its larger context.

In the case of Lucrece, Chaucer uses a similar technique to undermine the points he appears to be making in her favor. He includes a gratuitous reference to Saint Augustine, for example—ostensibly as someone who praises Lucrece. However, as Pat Trefzger Overbeck points out, "St. Augustine . . . passes judgment on Lucrece in his *City of God:* if you extenuate her homicide, you confirm the adultery; if you acquit her of adultery, you make the charge of homicide heavier; either way she is culpable."[67]

Amplification achieves its effect by including too much information rather than too little, but the end is the same: to worry the reader into questioning what is stated. With Lucrece, again, so much is made of her fainting during the rape—"She can feel nothing, either foul or fair"—that it seems to answer the unspoken charge that had she been awake she would have felt pleasure. This bizarre suspicion would probably never have been aroused if it had not been placated quite so vigorously.

Amplification reaches its height in the legend of Thisbe. Shakespeare made her and her lover Pyramus unredeemably silly in his *A Midsummer Night's Dream.* Those who have studied the legend, however, detect a hint of the ridiculous even in the earliest versions. Ovid's telling of their story may well aim at a humorous effect, since Ovid's sentimentality often masks a comic purpose. Chaucer's contemporary John Gower calls their story an example of "foolish haste." The double suicide is tellingly overdone both in Chaucer and in his Ovidian source. The sight (from Ovid) of blood flowing from Pyramus' wound like water from a broken pipe is undignified at best.

Thisbe's frenzied grief at finding Pyramus' body is told at so quick a pace (lines 861–881) that the action seems to be on fast-forward. In seven lines, she tears her hair, torments herself, lies swooning on the ground, weeps tears into his wound, and so on. Thisbe prefaces her own suicide with a warning to women not to follow her example: "Let no woman be so confident / As to take part in such an incident." The moral of the story, according to its heroine, is that women of good breeding should not follow their lovers into the woods at night.[68]

Chaucer's omissions and exaggerations appear in relief when his versions of the stories are held up against the traditionally accepted and familiar versions—the old reliable stories he lauds in the prologue. Again and again, a brief reference or extraneous detail calls to mind what he has left out, or suggests meanings different from those he claims. Another of the legends' ironic techniques lies in the poet's stated relationship to his sources. His task as dictated by Cupid and Alceste includes using old books, and he has professed his own devotion to books' authority. Yet only thirty lines into the first legend he qualifies his description of Mark Antony by saying that he was the equal of any man "unless the books lie."

The most marked questioning of authority occurs in the legend of Dido, whose story was surely the most familiar to Chaucer's audience. He begins by praising the name of Vergil and promising to follow that poet closely in telling Dido's story. In fact, however, he follows Ovid's version more closely. His assertion of slavish adherence to authority becomes even more humorous when one realizes that this legend does more overt challenging of its sources than any other. Chaucer hedges when confronted with Vergil's description of Aeneas entering Carthage:

> Aeneas through the town in secret passed,
> And when he came into the temple vast
> (I cannot say if possible it be)
> Venus gave him invisibility—
> Without a lie, the book tells it this way [lines 1018–1022].

He falters again when describing another of Venus' miracles, and this time fails to recover his stance as a believer:

> [Aeneas] is more than ever glad
> To see his little son Ascanius.
> However—for our author tells it thus—
> In the boy's place was Cupid, god of love,
> Who at the pleading of Venus above
> The likeness of the child agreed to take
> So that this noble lady he could make
> Enamored of Aeneas; though this may
> Be true, I hesitate myself to say.

In questioning Vergil as a source and Venus as a miracle-worker, Chaucer is undermining authority on two levels. Eleanor Leach comments, "where he might have scored points in Dido's favor by telling how her love, inspired by the gods, was no fault of her own, Chaucer lets his opportunity slip" (Leach, p. 153). By calling Vergil's authority into question, the narrator reveals a certain amount of rebellion against the demand that he follow old books. But much more rebellious is the poet's questioning of Venus' power in a work commanded by her son Cupid. In this instance, as in others, Chaucer's overt references to his sources signal departures from them or challenges to them.

Amplification, abbreviation, and distortion of sources also enable

Chaucer to turn a motley group of men into representatives of a fixed pattern. If the women are all to be innocent victims, the men—Aeneas, Pyramus, and Tarquin alike—must be villains. In order to make his point, the poet tells us repeatedly how devious and false men are as lovers. This stress on men's innate viciousness makes all their other qualities incidental. The sources may exalt them as heroes; Chaucer, however, plays down any elements of their stories that would divert attention from their unworthiness as lovers. Yet, from the women's point of view, these men possess irresistible attractions. In order to understand the good women's actions, we must look at their responses to these men.

Cleopatra loves Antony "for his chivalry"; unless books lie, he is the equal of any man in looks, rank, courage, and wisdom (lines 607–612). Pyramus is "one of the lustiest" young men in Babylon. Both of these men are also conveniently placed as potential lovers. Cleopatra gains great power for her Egyptian empire by winning the support of Antony. Thisbe surely loves Pyramus because he is one of the few men she has ever seen; Chaucer stresses the fact that women in Thisbe's nation and time were kept in seclusion. Behind many of the stories lurks the suspicion that the good women fall in love with certain men because they are the only men around, or because they have something to offer the women that other men do not. Sexual attraction is important as a motive, of course, but of at least equal importance are the power and prestige that will accrue to the wives of these men.

Aeneas we perceive through Dido's senses:

> [She] saw the man, how he was like a knight,
> And good enough in person and in might,
> And showing promise of nobility,
> And able to make speeches pleasingly,
> And, as it chanced, having a noble face,
> And bones and muscles formed for manly grace—
> Venus had given him such handsomeness
> That no man could be half so fair, I guess—
> And certainly a nobleman seemed he (lines 1066–1074).

Sight and seeing dominate these passages. Aeneas speaks well; he looks like a knight and a lover. The fact that he is a stranger (line 1075) makes him even more attractive. Aeneas, like many of the other men in the legends, has the gift of eliciting sympathy. His recent sufferings and his need of her have the most powerful attraction for Dido: "And soon her heart has pity of his woe, / And with that pity, love comes in also." Having the ability to help him, having every reason to expect his gratitude, Dido goes beyond the usual bounds of modesty and chaste reputation. Aeneas' "distress" reverses their roles, so that she can court him, make him lavish presents, give him the security usually offered by knights to ladies "in distress." Chaucer's Aeneas falls into the role of subservient courtly lover with ease. Vergil's hero becomes a sort of fop who waits upon his lady at feasts and dances; his deeds of arms at jousts are sandwiched between his songwriting and trinket-sending (lines 1261–1274). When he tires of the game, he makes plans to leave by night and carries them out, despite Dido's desperate pleas for him to stay.

Dido's desperation alerts us to a source of her passion beyond his physical prowess and charm. Dido finds (or thinks she finds) in Aeneas both a liege man, indebted and in her power, and a consort, able by birth and reputation to protect her and her realm. Whom could Dido marry so felicitously? If she married one of her subjects, she would lower herself in the eyes of the world. If she married one of the neighboring kings, her own sovereignty would be diminished. And, as we have seen, she must marry or remain chaste in order to survive at all. Her gifts and honors to Aeneas all go for the purpose of obliging him to marry her; the greatest is the gift of her chastity. But all her gifts fall short of their purpose; she cannot evoke enough gratitude to make him stay.

Jason, like Aeneas a stranger and guest in need of help, also exerts power over women by his looks, charm, and pitiable condition. A long and very telling list of the qualifications for a lover is presented by Hercules to Hypsipyle as qualities belonging to Jason. First, no man is half so true in love. Also, he possesses in abundance the qualities of generosity, vigor, and gentle birth. His only flaw, according to Hercules, comes from his excessive bashfulness and reluctance to be known as a lover. This endorsement contains some troubling discrepancies. No man exists who is half so true in love, Hercules says; but either Jason has not loved and so has not been tried, or has loved and so has not been true. Hercules' emphasis on Jason's hardiness, lustiness, generosity, and especially discretion seems to recommend him for an illicit relationship rather than for marriage. Yet, Hercules drops a mighty hint at the end of this passage that marriage is what Jason "needs."

Hercules, acting as pander for his friend, manipulates Hypsipyle's hopes and fears with cynical skill. Hercules knows and plays upon her vulnerabilities as a woman. He endows Jason with the characteristics both of an exciting lover and of a reliable husband, showing her what she has to gain. He also emphasizes Jason's absolute discretion, thus enabling her to forget what she has to lose. The bargain seems safe enough, the rewards great enough, for her to invest her chastity in order to obtain his love. She overlooks what Ovid's Dido calls "the penalty owed to shame." Yet this penalty, exacted when Jason sails away to the next love affair and leaves her with two children, admits her to the ranks of Cupid's martyrs.

After leaving Hypsipyle, Jason gains the love of Medea in order to obtain her help in his quest of the golden fleece. Again, with Medea, Jason's gift for making women love him lies in his looks, his renown, his speech, his ability to act like a lover, and—most of all—his dependence on her help. He promises marriage at exactly the right moment, after she has proved to him that only she can save him and before they have become lovers. Once she has staked her virginity on his promise, their roles reverse. He is in control, because she has literally given up everything for him.

Theseus, worst of all deceitful men, has one preeminent virtue: he is a king's son. This fact is mentioned six times in fewer than two hundred lines. His appearance receives slighter description than Jason's, but his persuasive rhetoric is shown in action. When he has the sympathetic attention of Ariadne, he swears to be her page and to live humbly in her service, while repeatedly mentioning his princely status. Ariadne responds just as he intends. She thinks that it would be a waste to let a lord's son die, and it is she who makes the suggestion of marriage. Theseus plays upon her romantic notions by "admitting" that he has loved her, sight unseen, for many years and has been wishing to see her "most of any creature." But his gift for seduction shows most clearly when, in four lines, he exalts her desirability, his own steadfastness, her dominance over him as a lover, and the rank she will attain by marriage with him:

> Upon my honor, then, to you I swear
> That seven years I've served you faithfully.
> Now I have you, and you also have me,
> My dearest one, of Athens the duchess! [lines 2119–2122]

The narrator, in an apostrophe to Theseus, voices the reasoning behind the apparently unreasoning passion of several of the good women. Theseus, in prison and soon to be sacrificed to the Minotaur, should be eternally grateful to anyone who would help him. Moreover, he should show this gratitude by pledging faithful love (lines 1954–1958).[69] We again see the force of expected gratitude, which gives women a false assurance of safety, in "The Legend of Phyllis." Leach points out how Chaucer expands upon Ovid's suggestion in the *Heroides* "that Demophoön came to her in need of material assistance, which she readily supplied." In Chaucer's version, Leach says, "Demophoön . . . arrives in graphic desperation nearly crushed by his encounter with a heavy storm" (Leach, p. 196). Phyllis has an apparently strong position from which to bargain for marriage. Chaucer abbreviates all description of their wooing to the business transaction at the heart of it: "Therefore to Phyllis he has promised thus / To wed her, and has sworn by all things good, / And then has stolen everything he could" (lines 2465–2467).

All these women—Dido, Hypsipyle, Medea, Ariadne, and Phyllis, half of Chaucer's list—place mistaken reliance upon what seems to be their advantageous position in relationship to their lovers. The measure of their expectations appears in their willingness to stake even their chastity. All the men promise faithful love as their part of the bargain, but their promises are short-lived. Among the good women, however, *trouthe* is the preeminent virtue. The Middle English word *trouthe* (from which modern *truth* and *troth*, as in *betrothal*, are derived) has several meanings. It is the making and keeping of bargains, one's word; it is also integrity, wholeness, faithfulness to self. The good women base their selfhood on *trouthe* in the sense of faithfulness and also of name, as when they are true to their vows of marriage and wifehood. They also depend upon *trouthe* in the sense of keeping bargains.

When their lovers betray them—breaking *trouthe*—they make a single-minded adherence to that broken bargain the touchstone of their existence. Thus, they attain the moral superiority exalted by the God of Love and by his poet Chaucer. Eleanor Leach and John Fyler, critics who have emphasized the rhetorical hyperbole of the *Legend*, see the elevation of "fallen" women as humorously revealing the inadequacy and falseness of the rhetorical devices and of the heroines themselves. That the women are not really admirable heroines makes the rhetoric of the *Legend* funny and reveals their vaunted *trouthe* to be very spurious indeed.

Although he does not absolve them of responsibility for their fates, Chaucer shows much sympathy for the betrayed women whose stories he tells so often. He has portrayed the "good woman" as an innocent *manqué*, misled by her belief that self-sacrifice will be rewarded or is its own reward. These women fail by risking too much, or rather, perhaps, by not risking enough, since they accept society's valuation of them even as they attempt to trade that valued commodity—chastity—for the security they desire. Like Christine de Pizan, Chaucer finds "such foolish love" a great danger to women, and reveals it as such. Unlike Christine, however, he holds out little hope for women who preserve their chastity for the sake of a reward—whether a husband or a good name. As he would do in *The Canterbury Tales*, Chaucer here seems to praise human diversity above any creed; in the *Legend,* though, he exalts diversity by showing the results of its absence.

The rejection of all other types of authority for that of romantic passion is for critic Pat Trefzger Overbeck the unifying aspect of all the good women, in the *Legend* and in other works by Chaucer. In her article "Chaucer's Good Woman" (mentioned above), she describes the "composite Good Woman." The Good Woman rejects divine authority: "In striking contrast to her prototype in the saint's legend and to her sister heroine in the medieval romance, Cupid's saint is deprived of, or spared, impelling supernatural motivations or influences, whether God, gods, Fate, or Fortune" (Overbeck, p. 77.) The women also reject human authority, both political and familial. Reigning queens—Cleopatra, Dido, Hypsipyle, and Phyllis—put aside the demands of the authority they themselves hold in order to pursue their lovers. For these women, "[t]he only meaningful authority is in the love relationship" (Overbeck, p. 78).

In freeing themselves from all other authority, however, the good women only make themselves more dependent upon the one form in which they invest all meaning. Overbeck says, "The prototypal Good Woman, free from the restraints of authority and the dictates of reason, pursues an *ignis fatuus,* a hallowed earthly union or a sublunary perfection impossible of attainment, destroying herself in the process" (p. 85). *Trouthe,* represented in the marriage vow, is the essential virtue for the good women because, in the first instance, they believe that it will obtain for them the lovers they desire; and because, in the second, it gives them a powerful sense of moral identity even more important than the lovers themselves.

This theme—the importance of the marriage vow or promise to marry—recurs throughout the legends. Being Aeneas' wife has such importance for Dido that she refers to it repeatedly when he speaks of leaving. She even asks Aeneas to marry her and then kill her, so that she can die as his wife (lines 1319–1322). Both Hypsipyle and Medea consider themselves to be Jason's wife. It is said of Hypsipyle that, despite Jason's desertion, she keeps herself chaste "as befit his wife"; she never again feels any happiness and eventually dies of grief. Lucrece kills herself out of what seems excessive reverence for wifely chastity. When her friends and family offer to forgive her for her loss of chastity in being raped, she answers them with punning forcefulness: "Of this forgiveness much ado you make; / Forgiveness is a gift I will not take." (Note the emphatic multiple negatives in Chaucer's words: "'Be as be may,' quod she, 'of forgyvyng, / I wol not have noo forgyft for nothing.'")

Hypermnestra, like Lucrece, may be said to carry her wifehood too far. She has gone through a marriage, arranged by their fathers, to a man she seems not to have known, although he is her first cousin. Told by her father to kill him, she debates with herself the course she should take:

> [H]e or I must surely lose our life.
> Now certainly, because I am his wife,
> And have my faith, better it is for me
> To meet my death in wifely honesty
> Than be a traitor living in my shame.

Here we have the virtue of all the good women reduced to its most essential qualities: it is a concept of self seen strictly in relation to society; its alternative is public disgrace; and it is not freely chosen. Hypermnestra does not claim to love her husband, but she acts as a wife is told she should, faithful and self-sacrificing even to a bond she did not choose. The only good woman who does not in some sense suffer for her marriage vows (or for the lack of them) is Philomela, who is raped by her sister's husband. Chaucer says of her that she suffered "for her sister's love." This enigmatic phrase suggests that Philomela's love for her sister led her to trust marriage vows that were not made to her but that betrayed her nevertheless.

FIGURE 3. Hypermnestra, from a French translation of *Heroides*, ca. 1500.
By permission of The British Library. Harley 4867f.108v.

THE LEGEND'S VICTIMS: THEIR MEANING AND EFFECT

Many feminist critics are looking again at images of women formerly called "victims" and are discovering what Nina Auerbach calls "new icons"—the "empowered outcast," the "disobedient woman."[70] Auerbach sees the Victorian imagination as endowing supposedly victimized women—in both literature and life—with a "demonic" power that far surpasses the might of her supposed oppressors. Jo Ann McNamara questions the idea that women in the early Church were victimized by men's fear of their sexuality; rather, she sees these women's rejection of their physical femaleness as enabling them to follow their own, freely chosen spiritual calling (see note 36 and discussion). French feminists Catherine Clément and Hélène Cixous debate whether the female hysteric, especially Freud's patient "Dora," is "a heroine or a victim."[71] Cixous empowers Dora by seeing her as "the name of a certain disturbing force which means that the little circus no longer runs" (Gallop, p. 134).

Can Chaucer's "good woman" also be seen by feminists as a heroine, capable, as Dora perhaps is, of bringing patriarchy's "little circus" to a halt? Chaucer's "good woman," like Auerbach's demonic woman, "breaks the boundaries of family within which her society restricts her" (Auerbach, p. 1); she "[defies] . . . the family, the patriarchal state, and God the Father" (p. 1). Chaucer's heroines have the power of royal lineage or actual queenship; of wealth; of beauty and sexual attractiveness; and often of intelligence (Phaedra) or even sorcery (Medea). And most of the good women—in the original versions of their stories, at least—commit or catalyze enough mayhem to shake family, society, and religion to the roots. Jason, Theseus, Tereus, and others among Chaucer's group of reviled seducers were at last punished viciously by the women they betrayed or by other women. Lucrece overthrew a whole system of government with her suicide.

Nevertheless, Chaucer's treatment of the women in the *Legend* is directed firmly and effectively at diminishing their power and their effect on the societies that repress them. Where he can, he omits their deeds of extravagant revenge and underplays the woeful effects of their actions on anyone but themselves. Again and again, his legends end with a woman destroyed, a man unscathed, a patriarchy strengthened. He also underplays the women's unique qualities, so that each good woman becomes a reiteration of those who have gone before and a prefiguration of those to come—some of whom he addresses in his audience. Chaucer divests his good women of their "demonic" power; and, as Overbeck points out, he lets them divest themselves of the rest. His vitiated heroines fall short of destructive grandeur, as they do of admirable virtue.

The rules governing life for the women of the *Legend* push them all to desperate actions and to tragic fates. The women themselves differ as much as women can: Lucrece and Philomela, cruelly raped; Hypermnestra, forced into marriage and then into the choice of murder or virtual suicide; Medea and Cleopatra, goaded by their passion into infamous crimes. The fact that in the end they resemble each other so completely is, I think, meant to shock us. The *Legend* exaggerates the implicit message of the catalogue and of much other writing about women; in doing so, it makes us see more clearly what we might have taken for granted. In this case, we see that women cannot be spoken of as a moral entity governed by one absolute standard.

The *Legend* derives much of its effectiveness from the relationship it builds between the narrator, the world of the poem, and the world of the audience.[72] The prologue suggestively portrays the poem's audience as the enclosed, ordered, and gracious world of the court—a court modeled on the "courts of love," and equally fictional. The narrator mentions the contest between the flower and the leaf, which provided a backdrop for love debates. Alceste, in the F-version of the prologue, requests presentation of the finished poem to the queen. The narrator addresses his audience of young lovers, asking them to help him with his rhyming. These details encourage us to envision the audience as made up of the "young, fresh folk" addressed at the ending of *Troilus*. Yet the audience is warned from the outset, and with increasing frequency as the legends continue, against making a comfortable identification with the lovers of the *Legend*. The identification that Chaucer prompts would be deeply uncomfortable if it were not comic: all men are faithless deceivers, all women are destroyed by love. Cupid tells the narrator that it is now considered a game for men to shame as many women as possible. Alceste directs him to tell the stories of false men who betray women. The legends amplify these warnings. The story of Cleopatra ends with the narrator saying,

> Until I find a man so true and stable,
> Who will for love his death so freely take,
> I pray to God our heads may never ache!

The story of Pyramus and Thisbe contains one of the few good men the narrator says he has found in all his books; nevertheless, both the narrator and Thisbe warn women against trusting their reputations and safety to men. Chaucer's third retelling of the story of Dido repeats this warning. The narrator speaks out to address women in the audience, saying that not only old examples but their own observations should warn them against men.

Addresses to true and trusting women and to false men appear in the *Legend* with increasing frequency and exaggeration. Describing Jason, the narrator says he does not have time to tell about his wooing, "But if in this house a false lover be, / Exactly as he now does, so did he" (lines 1554–1555). Men are not to be trusted. A man will not be faithful to one woman unless he can obtain no other (lines 2387–2393). Men are "the subtle foe," so that women, the narrator says, should trust in love "no man but me" (line 2561). The "morals" here have become as extreme as their opposites, the warnings of misogynists like Jerome against women. In fact, substitute "women" for "men" and they say exactly the same things.

Chaucer has followed Cupid's instructions and redressed the wrongs of antifeminist writing, though he has done so in ways that the god would be unlikely to appreciate. He has praised a number of women, some "deserving" in Cupid's terms, some not; and he has dispraised men so excessively as to make any such generalization about either sex seem ludicrous. The fact that he addresses so many of his warnings against men to his imagined audience of young lovers who, if they were to take him seriously, would surely feel uncomfortable helps to defuse those warnings. Yet, by preaching against a whole gender, he recreates an experience that must have been familiar to the women in his audience. In so doing, he reveals the folly of such practices. The *Legend* argues forcefully against moral absolutes by creating a world over which they hold tyrannical sway, with results that are far from moral. The good women are not real women but distortions; they follow a pattern of ideal womanhood and demonstrate its dangers. In this way, they reveal the pattern itself to be the source of distortion.

AFTERWORD

What of the women who read the catalogues of good women? Medieval literature and history have little to say of their reactions.[73] Christine de Pizan, as we have seen, exhorted women to be chaste, not only for the sake of virtue but as a practical measure for self-protection. Yet centuries of reading about the virtues of wifely devotion and womanly sacrifice were surely not without influence on the lives of real women. Chaucer's *Canterbury Tales* contains two women who show some measure of self-awareness regarding the myths that shape their lives. In Dorigen and the Wife of Bath, Chaucer offers telling commentary on the power that art wields over life. In them, too, he offers what can be seen as a direct appraisal of the dangers that "good women" pose for real women. Foreshadowing Virginia Woolf, both these women find they must kill the "angel" of mythical female virtue in order to preserve their lives and integrity.

The Example of Dorigen: "To Be Dead in Wifely Innocence"

Dorigen in Chaucer's *Franklin's Tale* conceives of her role as wife in the most idealistic terms. When her husband has to be away, she behaves like a romance heroine: weeping, sighing, mourning, lying awake, wailing, fasting, complaining, losing all joy in life. Dorigen again acts the romance heroine when a young knight, Aurelius, declares his love for her. She agrees to love him if he can make the dangerous rocks in the surrounding sea disappear. Her essential fidelity to Arveragus is not swayed. The rocks worry her because they endanger him; moreover, she believes the talk to be impossible and plainly tells Aurelius that he is foolish to pursue her. Her rash promise represents no more than indulgence in melancholic fantasy. She does not really believe herself to be the heroine of a romance, though from time to time she acts like one. Much to her surprise, she finds out later that she is indeed living in a world of romance. The rocks disappear.

Forced to confront the ideals of behavior with which she has been entertaining herself, Dorigen turns first to examples of noble wives from literature—specifically, from Jerome. Reciting a long list of martyrs to chastity, whose example she intends to follow, she begins with women who died rather than lose their virtue. It is a strong beginning. She employs apostrophes, rhetorical questions, interjections, and quotations in telling the stories of many such martyrs. She arrives at the bottom of the heap with rather oblique references to Bilyea, whose virtue consisted in not telling her old husband that he had bad breath;

Rodogune, who killed her nurse for suggesting that she remarry; and Teuta, Artemesia, and Valeria, who, though often mentioned as examples of good women, do not fit the announced contents of this catalogue.

Dorigen's thesis—that many wives and maidens have killed themselves rather than lose their honor—presents a deceptively simple choice between death and dishonor. As the examples are from Jerome, so this choice reflects the ideal of chastity as propounded by Jerome and his confreres. The self-destructive acts of these women have much the same flavor as those of the *Legend*'s martyrs; Lucrece and Alceste appear in both catalogues.

Certain phrases used by the Franklin emphasize the fact that Dorigen behaves as would a fictional lady when confronted with a separation from her lover, a suit from a would-be lover, a challenge to her virtue. Rather than reinforcing the fictionality of Dorigen, the comparison conveys the reality of her situation. She is accustomed, as many noblewomen must have been, to modeling her reactions and her behavior on the examples of ideal women from mythology, history, and romance. When the loss of her virtue seems imminent, the examples urge her to kill herself.

Through the Franklin's bourgeois good sense, Chaucer shows us a woman trying to follow "noble" models of virtue that are inhumane in the extreme. *The Legend of Good Women,* a virtual encyclopedia of such rules and models, makes the same point in a different way. *The Franklin's Tale* dramatizes in the realm of experience (albeit fictional experience) the effects of this kind of authority upon those who try to follow it. Dorigen, a much fuller and more complex woman than the heroines of the *Legend,* gains our sympathy when she tries to follow their example of perfection—and turns back once she realizes the cost.

The Example of the Wife of Bath: "Who Painted the Lion?"

The Wife of Bath is among those of Chaucer's pilgrims who seem so real that scholars have tried to locate the historical personages they represent. Chaucer wove her complex fabric from many strands: she is the lusty and practical Dame Nature from *The Romance of the Rose,* the fearsome shrewish wife from antifeminist satire, the sexually attractive and voracious woman from *fabliau* humor. Her much-married state represents Saint Jerome's worst fears. She is, in herself, a whole catalogue of bad women brought to unrepentant life.

As one might expect, a woman who combines all the vices that anti-feminists can devise is not one to be subdued when their weapons are turned against her. Rather, she puts their weapons to her own use. In Alice of Bath, Chaucer delivers yet another blow to those who would legislate women's morality without consulting the women themselves. He creates a woman who knows antifeminist teachings well, and he makes her possession of this knowledge believable by showing that she has had it preached to her, by church and by husbands, for most of her life. He creates in her a character sensitive enough to care about these teachings, strong enough to go against them, and intelligent enough to defend her choice.

The Wife of Bath does not try to prove by example that all women are good, or that even one woman is perfect. She is willing to admit her faults but insists that her enemies be detected in theirs. Like them, she is willing to descend to broad satire to make her points. A typical anti-feminist "proverb" would be one her fifth husband quotes to her: "A fair woman, unless she is also chaste, is like a gold ring in a sow's nose." [74] To this, compare her own adage regarding "clerks":

> The clerk, when he is old and cannot do
> In works of Venus worth his worn-out shoe,
> Sits down and writes, in his senility,
> How wives can't keep their vows of chastity.

Of these verbal missiles, hers is the more effective, because it places the source of men's bitterness against women in the men's own insufficiency. (It is also much funnier.)

The stories of catalogue-makers, read to her at length by her fifth husband, depress and anger the Wife of Bath. Although women have more to complain of in men than the reverse, she says, women get all the blame because men write all the books. Of the abundance of anti-feminist stories, she asks, "Who painted the lion?" The question refers to the fable of Aesop in which a painting shows a hunter killing a lion. The lion who looks at the painting knows that, had it been painted by a lion, the situation would have been reversed. Although she asks this question of the overtly misogynistic stories that accuse women of every possible vice, she could equally well ask it of the catalogues of "good women" that limit women's possible virtues to chastity and self-destruction.

In her prologue and tale—and, she would have her listeners believe, in her life—the Wife of Bath takes every opportunity to wrest power from complacent men and turn it to her own uses. She says she wants to be a true and loving wife, but from her own choice and on her own terms, not because she is forced. Her fate in recent criticism has often borne out her own belief that the men who wrote the stories have secured their superior position. Some critics turn to the very writers she refutes for proof that Chaucer meant the Wife of Bath to be understood as a cautionary example of women's vices.

Nevertheless, the Wife of Bath surely must speak for many women subjected to the barrage of antifeminist propaganda, in her time and in all the others: "Who would have guessed, or who would have supposed / The sorrow that was in my heart, and pain?"

1. See Lisa J. Kiser, *Telling Classical Tales* (Ithaca, N.Y.: Cornell University Press, 1983), especially pp. 101–111; and John M. Fyler, *Chaucer and Ovid* (New Haven: Yale University Press, 1979), especially pp. 98–99, 101.

2. The God of Love gives instructions in the prologue regarding the ladies whose stories Chaucer is to tell. He requests that Chaucer "have in mind" the women named in the *balade*—there are eighteen—plus Alceste.

3. Chaucer's narrator, or persona, is the poet's depiction of himself as speaker of and character in his works. See E. Talbot Donaldson, "Chaucer the Pilgrim," reprinted in Donaldson's *Speaking of Chaucer* (New York: W. W. Norton, 1972), *passim*.

4. Many historical and occasional interpretations have been offered for the *Legend*, most focusing on the identification of Alceste as one or another royal lady at whose request Chaucer was writing. A useful overview of these interpretations can be found in John Fisher's chapter, "*The Legend of Good Women*," in *Companion to Chaucer Studies*, ed. Beryl Rowland (New York: Oxford University Press, 1979), pp. 464–76, especially pp. 464–70. According to Fisher, the identification of Alceste as Queen Anne is the oldest (first made by Lydgate around 1435) and most common (p. 465).

5. For a thorough discussion of this question, see Robert Worth Frank, Jr., *Chaucer and The Legend of Good Women* (Cambridge, Mass.: Harvard University Press, 1972), pp. 189–210; see also Kiser, *Telling Classical Tales*, pp. 95–97.

6. "Chaucer's *Legend of Good Women*," *Journal of English and Germanic Philology* 7 (1908): 87–129 and 8 (1909): 47–111.

7. John Livingston Lowes, "Is Chaucer's *Legend of Good Women* a Travesty?" *Journal of English and Germanic Philology* 8 (1909): 513–69.

8. Ph.D. diss., Yale University, 1963.

9. *Chaucer Review* 2 (1967): 84, 75–94.

10. V. A. Kolve, "From Cleopatra to Alceste: An Iconographic Study

of *The Legend of Good Women,*" in *Signs and Symbols in Chaucer's Poetry,* ed. John P. Hermann and John J. Burke, Jr. (University, Ala.: University of Alabama Press, 1977), pp. 130–78. An exception to this critical tendency to ignore the stated subject is found in Elaine Tuttle Hansen's "Irony and the Antifeminist Narrator in Chaucer's *Legend of Good Women,*" *Journal of English and Germanic Philology* 82 (1983): 11–31. Tuttle sees the poem's tone as "systematically and profoundly ironic" (p. 12), its "irony . . . directed . . . at Cupid, at the narrator . . . , and at the antifeminist tradition to which both . . . subscribe" (p. 12).

11. Kiser, *Telling Classical Tales;* see my annotated bibliography; and Russell A. Peck, "Chaucerian Poetics and the Prologue to the *Legend of Good Women,*" in *Chaucer in the Eighties,* ed. Julian N. Wasserman and Robert J. Blanch (Syracuse: Syracuse University Press, 1986), pp. 39–55.

12. Delany, Diamond, and Hansen presented papers on the *Legend* at the Fifth International Congress of the New Chaucer Society, March 20–23, 1986, in Philadelphia. Delany sees the *Legend* as showing women equated with nature, turned into signs. "The Prologue constructs an aesthetic of nature, in which nature and language are linked through a series of images and scenes whose thrust is the 'natural' fidelity of signifier to signified—a fidelity threatened by the God of Love's demand for an inaccurate picture of women" (unpublished abstract, p. 6). Diamond says that the models of women's virtue proposed by the *Legend* are neither fulfilled nor fully undermined. Echoes of the saints' lives, in which virgin martyrs confront male authority, show the good women and their virtue by contrast to be false and unavailing. Diamond warns against an ironic reading of the *Legend,* arguing that irony is in the eye of the beholder and is too often used to confirm the reader's own preferences. Hansen sees the *Legend* as being concerned with the feminization of men as lovers and as love poets, and she urges reconsideration of the view of Chaucer himself as a feminist or humanist.

13. "Myths," writes Elizabeth Janeway, "attempt to explain the world out there to ourselves" and "to manipulate the world." *Man's World, Woman's Place* (New York: Morrow, 1971), p. 295.

14. Marina Warner, *Joan of Arc: The Image of Female Heroism* (New York: Knopf, 1981), p. 9.

15. *Patrologiae cursus completus, ser. Latina* (Paris: J.-P. Migne, 1890), 23, col. 294.

16. *The Book of the City of Ladies,* trans. Earl Jeffrey Richards (New York: Persea Books, 1982), p. 155.

17. *The Aeneid of Vergil,* trans. Allen Mandelbaum (New York: Bantam Books, 1971), p. 91.

18. *The Aeneid of Virgil,* Books I–VI, ed. R. D. Williams (1972; reprint ed., New York: St. Martin's Press, 1977), Book IV, line 322, p. 84. Translations are mine.

19. This definition of *pudendum* is the first listed by the *American Heritage Dictionary* (Boston: Houghton Mifflin, 1976).

20. For the modern romance novel's function as wish-fulfillment, see Janice Radway, *Reading the Romance* (Chapel Hill: University of North Carolina Press, 1984).

21. These three types are sketched by Francis Lee Utley in *The Crooked Rib* (Columbus: Ohio State University Press, 1944), p. 44.

22. Utley, *The Crooked Rib,* p. 44. See also Kiser's discussion of *exempla, Telling Classical Tales,* pp. 78–81, 93–94, and 98–102; and Fyler, *Chaucer and Ovid,* p. 114.

23. Hesiod, *Homeric Hymns and Homerica,* intro. and trans. Hugh Evelyn-White (Cambridge, Mass.: Harvard University Press, 1914), p. xxii.

24. Homer, *The Odyssey,* trans. Robert Fitzgerald (New York: Anchor Books, 1963), p. 192.

25. Euripides, *Electra,* in *Medea and Other Plays,* trans. Philip Vellacott (1963; reprint ed., New York: Penguin Books 1982), p. 140. This is Clytemnestra's statement of her own motives.

26. *Aeneid,* ed. Williams, Book VI, lines 445–449, p. 139.

27. *Oxford Classical Dictionary,* 2d ed., ed. N. G. L. Hammond and H. H. Scullard (Oxford: Clarendon Press, 1970).

28. Dido speaks of feeling "the traces of an old flame" ("*veteris vestigia flammae*") when she falls in love with Aeneas after her long widowhood (*Aeneid,* ed. Williams, Book IV, line 23, p. 74).

29. Jaques Perret, "Les compagnes de Didon aux enfers," *Revues et études latines* 42 (1964): 247. Translations are mine.

30. Ovid, *Metamorphoses* (Cambridge, Mass.: Harvard University Press, 1914), Book I, p. 194. My translation.

31. Howard Jacobson, *Ovid's Heroides* (Princeton: Princeton University Press, 1974), p. 349.

32. Ovid, *Heroides and Amores* (Cambridge, Mass.: Harvard University Press, 1914), Book I, lines 69–70, p. 14. Translations are mine.

33. Eleanor Winsor Leach, "The Sources and Rhetoric of Chaucer's 'Legend of Good Women' and Ovid's 'Heroides'" (Ph.D. diss., Yale University, 1963), p. 252.

34. Katharine M. Rogers, *The Troublesome Helpmate: A History of Misogyny in Literature* (Seattle: University of Washington Press, 1961), pp. 21, 22.

35. Sarah B. Pomeroy, *Goddesses, Whores, Wives, and Slaves: Women in Classical Antiquity* (New York: Schocken Books, 1975), p. 8.

36. For a thoughtful discussion of chastity in the early Church and of Jerome's attitude toward women in theory and reality, see Jo Ann McNamara, "Cornelia's Daughters: Paula and Eustochium," *Women's Studies* 11 (1984): 21.

37. Geoffrey Chaucer, *The Works of Geoffrey Chaucer*, 2d ed., ed. Fred N. Robinson (Boston: Houghton Mifflin, 1961), explanatory note, p. 840.

38. Giovanni Boccaccio, *Concerning Famous Women*, trans. and intro. Guido A. Guarino (London: George Allen and Unwin, 1964), pp. xxxviii–viv.

39. Boccaccio frequently satirized women, even in his romances. See Hope Phyllis Weissman, "Antifeminism and Chaucer's Characterizations of Women," in *Geoffrey Chaucer,* ed. George Economou (New York: McGraw-Hill, 1975), p. 98.

40. Christine de Pizan, *The Book of the City of Ladies,* trans. Earl Jeffrey Richards (New York: Persea Books, 1982), p. 155.

41. Susan Groag Bell, "Christine de Pizan (1364–1430): Humanism and the Problem of a Studious Woman," *Feminist Studies* 3 (1976): 177.

42. For good discussions of Chaucer's ironic technique, see Leach, "Sources and Rhetoric," *passim;* Elaine Tuttle Hansen, "Irony and the Antifeminist Narrator in Chaucer's *Legend of Good Women,*" *Journal of English and Germanic Philology* 82 (1983): *passim;* Robert Worth Frank, Jr., *Chaucer and the Legend of Good Women* (Cambridge, Mass.: Harvard University Press,

1972), pp. 96–123; and Kiser, *Telling Classical Tales,*
pp. 95–98.

43. For another example of antifeminist "praise" of women, see
Chaucer's *Merchant's Tale.* January unwittingly reveals his own
conception of women's virtue as their ability to serve his needs.

44. Chaucer wrote two versions of the prologue. The following discussion will refer to both unless indicated. For general discussion
of the two prologues, see Fisher, "The Legend of Good Women,"
pp. 464–70. Hansen argues that the revised "G" version "emphasizes the inherent antifeminism in the Religion of Love, at
least as Cupid here understands and articulates its doctrine"
(p. 13).

45. For historical interpretations, see Fisher, "The Legend of Good
Women," pp. 464–70.

46. Fyler, *Chaucer and Ovid,* p. 115, points out that, in context, the
Legend is a palinode—that is, a work written specifically as a
retraction of statements made in another work—in this case for
Troilus.

47. E. Talbot Donaldson, *Chaucer's Poetry* (New York: Ronald Press,
1975), p. 1122.

48. For critics who have written on the influence of the *marguerite*
poems, see Fisher, "The Legend of Good Women," pp. 464–70.

49. Ovid, *Metamorphoses,* trans. Mary M. Innes (1955; reprint ed.,
Baltimore: Penguin Books, 1975), pp. 72–73.

50. Edgar Wind, *Pagan Mysteries in the Renaissance,* rev. ed. (New
York: Norton, 1968), p. 115, describes how the story of her transformation, from Ovid's *Fasti,* is dramatized pictorially in Bot-
ticelli's *Primavera.*

51. Fyler, *Chaucer and Ovid,* p. 99.

52. Her name is revealed at an earlier point in the "G" version of the
prologue by the narrator, who seems to recognize her.

53. Ovid, *Metamorphoses,* trans. Innes, pp. 100–101.

54. "F" version, lines 291–299. In the "G" version, these ladies sing
the *balade* to the daisy.

55. Kiser, *Telling Classical Tales,* p. 130, differentiates between Alceste's "devoted husband" and the "unworthy" men in the legends. I would argue that Admetus' devotion is questionable in the
sources—he let her die, after all!—and goes unmentioned in the
Legend.

56. Peck argues that "Chaucer would have been among men [on his visits to Italy] who very likely knew the contents of the *Symposium* and may well have been talking about it" (p. 41), though he admits that "it is questionable how detailed Chaucer's knowledge of the contents of the dialogue could have been" (p. 41).

57. Plato, *Euthyphro, Apology, Crito, and Symposium*, trans. Jowett, rev. Moses Hadas (1953; reprint ed., Chicago: Henry Regnery, 1967), p. 87.

58. Plato, *Euthyphro, Apology, Crito, and Symposium*, p. 123.

59. Euripides, *Alcestis*, in *Euripides I*, ed. David Grene and Richard Lattimore (New York: Modern Library, 1955), p. 27.

60. Some readers see a symbolic message in the *Legend*'s account of the daisy's and Alceste's death and rebirth. Alceste is likened to Christ (rebirth) and to Mary (intercession). See, for example, V. A. Kolve, "From Cleopatra to Alceste: An Iconographic Study of *The Legend of Good Women*, in *Signs and Symbols in Chaucer's Poetry*, ed. John P. Hermann and John J. Burke, Jr. (University, Ala.: University of Alabama Press, 1977), pp. 130–78, and Kiser, *Telling Classical Tales*, pp. 47–48.

61. See especially Frank, *Chaucer and the Legend of Good Women*, who discusses the legends as experiments in different narrative styles.

62. Leach, "Sources and Rhetoric," pp. 42ff. See also Kiser, *Telling Classical Tales*, pp. 99–101; and Frank, *Chaucer and the Legend of Good Women*, pp. 199–210.

63. Beverly Taylor, "The Medieval Cleopatra: The Classical and Medieval Tradition of Chaucer's *Legend of Cleopatra*," *Journal of Medieval and Renaissance Studies* 7 (1977): 249–69; see also Fyler, *Chaucer and Ovid*, p. 100, and Hansen, "Irony," pp. 15–18.

64. Fyler, *Chaucer and Ovid*, p. 107, points out that this and other omissions weaken the heroines: "the preconceived pattern of sanctity defeats its own intent by enervating female heroism."

65. See ibid., p. 104.

66. See ibid., pp. 104–105.

67. Pat Trefzger Overbeck, "Chaucer's Good Woman," *Chaucer Review* 2 (1967): 84. See also Leach, "Sources and Rhetoric," p. 127.

68. Hansen, "Irony," pp. 18–21, discusses in detail Chaucer's treat-

ment of Thisbe, especially the effect of her address to the audience in the penultimate lines of the *Legend*. Hansen points out that "the universal terms of her advice . . . imply that all women are doomed in their attempts to escape social constraints on their sexual and emotional freedom" (p. 19).

69. Fyler points out (*Chaucer and Ovid*, p. 102) that Chaucer has emended his source by having Phaedra come up with the plan and Ariadne take the credit. See also Hansen, "Irony," p. 24. Perhaps Theseus' abandonment of Ariadne for Phaedra serves some sort of justice in Chaucer's version of the story.

70. Nina Auerbach, *Woman and the Demon: The Life of a Victorian Myth* (Cambridge, Mass.: Harvard University Press, 1982), p. 2.

71. Jane Gallop, *The Daughter's Seduction: Feminism and Psychoanalysis* (Ithaca: Cornell University Press, 1982), p. 133.

72. Kiser, *Telling Classical Tales,* pp. 98ff, traces these "direct statements of applicability" to the narrative technique of the saints' lives.

73. Christine de Pizan, of course, does express a woman's reaction to the ideas of misogyny and courtly love (which she calls "fol amor"). For two attempts to discover women's own views on these theories about them, see Elizabeth Hanson-Smith, "A Woman's View of Courtly Love: The Findern Anthology," *Journal of Women's Studies in Literature* 1 (1979): 179–94; and Ann McMillan, "'Fayre Sisters Al': *The Flower and the Leaf* and *The Assembly of Ladies*," *Tulsa Studies in Women's Literature* 1 (1982): 27–42.

74. Chaucer, *Works,* ed. Robinson, p. 83. My translation.

PART II

THE LEGEND OF GOOD WOMEN

PROLOGUE[1]

More than a thousand times I've heard men tell   (F 1–16)[2]
That there is joy in heaven and pain in hell,
And gladly I agree that it is so;
Nevertheless, this much I also know:
That none of those who in this country dwell
Has been himself to either heaven or hell
Or knows of it in any other way
Than reading books or hearing what men say.
Nobody can come back to testify.
But God forbid that people should deny
The truth of what they have not seen befall.
Even Bernard the monk[3] did not see all!
Nor should men rush to call a thing deceit
Because they may have happened not to see it.
If they themselves have failed to see or do
A thing, that doesn't mean it isn't true.

So we must go to old books that we find   (17–28)
Through which past incidents are kept in mind;
And to wise ancients we should pay heed now
(At least as far as reason will allow)
Who tell authoritative histories
Of saints, of kingdoms, and of victories,
Of love, of hate—so many things, I fear,
I must refrain from mentioning them here.
For if old books should ever cease to be,
With them we'd lose the key to memory.
To old books we must give the credit due—
Where there's no other proof, let's think them true.

And as for me, though what I know is slight,   (29–44)
Perusing these old books is my delight;
I give them faith, and trust, and reverence
So heartily, nothing can pull me thence—
No game can ever part my books and me
(Save Sundays[4]—even then, infrequently).

But one exception is the month of May;
Its coming is a special holiday.
When once again I hear the birds all sing,
And all the kinds of flowers start to spring,
Farewell my book, farewell my dedication!
And then I have a special inclination:
Of all the flowers blooming in the field,
To flowers red and white most love I yield—
Daisies, as they are called by people here—
This kind I hold particularly dear.

(45–65) So, as I said before, when it is May,
I'm not still in my bed at break of day,
But up and walking as the sun grows bright
To see its petals open to the light
As it awakens in the early morrows.
That blissful vision softens all my sorrows.
So I am glad, whenever I am near it,
To do all that I can do to revere it,
For she is, as it were, the flower of flowers,
And filled with virtuous and noble powers,
And ever the same is fair, and fresh of hue,
And ever the same I love it, old as new,
And always will, until my heart shall die.
Although I do not swear, I will not lie;
No hotter love was felt by anyone.
And when the evening starts to fall, I run,
Just as the sun is sinking in the west,
To see this flower as it goes to rest,
For she hates darkness, and she fears the night,
And lifts her full face only to the light.
When sun is shining, then she will unclose.

(66–96) Alas, I have no English, rhyme or prose,
That's good enough to praise this flower well.
But you with skill and cunning, help me tell—
You lovers, who can write of tender feeling,
Help me, it is to you I am appealing;
To aid my work you should be diligent.

Because you know my efforts are well-meant,
You ought to help me somewhat in this art,
Whether with leaf or flower⁵ you take part.
Of poetry you've harvested the best
Of all the grain, and I pick up the rest.
I'm lucky if I find an ear that's sound
Of words that you have let fall to the ground.
And if I might reuse a verse or two
Of some song that was first composed by you,
Be patient, for you know that I mean well,
And wish to honor love by what I tell.

This flower, too, I serve as best I might.
She is the only true and shining light
That steers me rightly in this dark world here.
You hold the heart within my breast with fear,
With love; and with such power it is done
That you have all myself, and I have none.
My word, my work, is knit so in your band
That as we see the harp obey the hand
Which makes it sound with careful fingering,
Just in this way, out of my heart you bring
A voice, just as you choose, to laugh or sigh;
Be you my guide and lady, till I die!
And to you as a god on earth I call,
Both in this work and in my sorrows all.

But to the cause I speak of—the promotion   (97–124)
Of credence in old books, and of devotion,
And the belief that faith should supplement
What senses and experience present—
That I shall speak of, when I see my time;
I cannot put it all at once in rhyme.
My busy spirit, thirsting always new
To see this flower, young and fresh of hue,
Compelled me with so burning a desire
That even now I still can feel the fire
That made me rise, before it yet was day—
This was the morning of the first of May—

My heart combining awe and glad affection—
To be a witness to the resurrection
Of this my flower, as it would unclose
Its petals to the sun, as red as rose,
That in the breast was of the beast,[6] that day,
That bore Agenor's daughter far away.[7]
And down upon my knees I went before it
And greeted this fresh flower, to adore it;
Till it had opened, I remained there kneeling
On grasses sweet to smell, and soft to feeling,
Embroidered all about with flowers sweet,
Of such sweetness and fragrance all complete
That there is none among the herbs and trees
But by comparison would fail to please.
For its perfume surpasses all the rest,
And above all its beauty is the best.

(125–170) The Earth had now forgotten its poor life
In winter, that wields coldness like a knife
And leaves the naked world exposed to grief,
Now that the kinder sun had brought relief
And all that had been bare was newly clad.
The small birds, which are in this season glad
For their escape from nets and traps of men
Think in despite to pay them back again
For causing fear and loss among their kind.
And thus they have defiance most in mind—
To sing against the fowler's treachery,
The churlish wretch that, with his sophistry
And selfishness, would gladly have them die.
This was their song: "The fowler we defy
And all his craft." And some of them sang clear
Verses of love, that were a joy to hear,
In honor of their mates, and in their praise;
And for the joy of blissful summer days,
On branches full of blossoms soft as feather
In their delight each couple came together
And sang, "A blessing on Saint Valentine,[8]

For on this day I choose you to be mine,
And never shall repent the choice, my sweet!"

And with these words their beaks began to meet
Yielding the honor and obeisance due
To love—they did their other duties too,
All that pertains to love and nature free;
Think what you please, you get no more of me.
And those of them who'd lapsed in their devotions,
As does the tidy,[9] with newfangled notions,
Begged mercy of their mates for doing wrong,
And humbly pledged repentance in their song,
And swore on blossoms they would sin no more
If their old mates would take them as before.
And at the last they came to one accord.
At first, they found Reluctance to be lord;
But Pity, through his strong and gentle might,
Forgave, enforcing Mercy over Right,
Through Innocence and Graceful Manners' rules.
Not that their innocence was that of fools,
Their pity false; the mean is virtue's source,
As *Ethics*[10] says; this kind I mean, of course.[11]
And thus these birds, free of maliciousness,
Agreed to love, and leave off viciousness,
And all began to sing of one accord,
"Welcome to summer, governor and lord!"

Zephyr and Flora,[12] with their gentle powers
And tender might, breathed out upon the flowers
Their breath, that sweetly urges them to swell,
The god and goddess of the flowery dell
In which I thought I might, day after day,
Dwell always, through the lovely month of May,
Forgetting sleep, forgoing meat and drink.
Gently, I let myself begin to sink
Down on my elbow, lying on the grass,
My mind made up to let the whole day pass
While I (and this is no exaggeration)

(171–196)

Gave to the daisy all my concentration,
Which with good reason has from men the name
"Daisy" or "Eye of Day" (they mean the same).[13]
Empress and flower of all flowers is she;
I pray that she may have prosperity,
And for her sake all flower-lovers thrive.
Nevertheless, do not think that I strive
To praise the flower and oppose the leaf,[14]
Or praise the corn and denigrate the sheaf.
I favor neither in their competition,
And neither furthers me in my ambition.
Who serves on either side I could not tell,
But hope their services reward them well.
For what I tell of has an older date,
Before their parties had begun debate.

(197–225)   At evening, when the sun sank in the west,
And when this flower folded for her rest
Because she dreads the darkness of the night,
I hastened home as quickly as I might
To sleep, and get up early as before,
To see this flower opening once more.
And in an arbor I have planted there,
With fresh-cut turfs arranged as benches fair,
I had my men make up a couch for me;
To celebrate the season's gaiety,
I told them to strew flowers on the bed;
And I lay down, and covered up my head.

I fell asleep there, in about two hours,
And dreamed about the meadow full of flowers;
It seemed that I was lying as before
Watching this flower that I so adore,
When, looking up, I saw from far away,
Yet coming toward the place in which I lay,
The God of Love, and on his arm a queen,
And she was wearing royal robes of green.
She wore upon her hair a golden net,
And over that a crown of white was set,

With tiny petals that, for all the world,
Looked like a daisy when it is unfurled—
For as a daisy is with petals crowned,
Just so these little flowers clustered round.
One pearl made up this crown, without division,
So that she seemed a daisy to my vision,
The net of gold forming the flower's core.

Of silk were the rich clothes that Cupid wore,   (226–248)
Embroidered in a green and red design
Where sprays of leaves and roses intertwined,
The freshest since the world was first begun.
To crown his golden hair he wore a sun,
Much lighter and more delicate than wire.
It seemed to me his face shone like a fire,
And I could scarcely look, it was so bright.
But what I could make out was worth the sight:
He held a pair of arrows, ember-red;
His wings, like angels', on each side were spread.
And even though men say he cannot see,
Nevertheless it seemed he looked at me;
The look he cast on me was so severe
That I could feel my heart grow cold with fear.
And by the hand he held this noble queen,
Crowned all in gold and white, and dressed in green,
So womanly, so pleasant, and so meek
That in this world, however far men seek,
They will not come on beauty half so rare
In any creature living anywhere.
And thus I now may say, most fittingly,
This song in praise of her nobility:

Balade[15]

Hide, Absalom, thy hair of golden sheen;   (249–269)
Esther, let all thy meekness fall from thee;
Hide, Jonathan, thine amiable mien;
Cato's wife Marcia, and Penelope,

Do not compare your wifely dignity.
Hide, Helen and Isolde, your beauties fine;
My lady comes, who may all these outshine.

Thy lovely body, let it not appear,
Lavinia; Lucrece, whom Romans claim,
Polyxena, who paid for love so dear,
And Cleopatra, with your passion's flame,
Hide you your faithful love and honored name;
And Thisbe, to whom love was so malign;
My lady comes, who may all these outshine.

Hero, Laodamia, Dido, hush;
Phyllis, who for Demophoön did die;
And Canace, marked by a guilty blush; [16]
Hypsipyle, by Jason left to cry;
Your faithfulness you must not praise so high;
Adrian, Hypermnestra, stand in line;
My lady comes, who may all these outshine.

(270–281) My lady, of all ladies on the earth,
Deserves well this balade to praise her worth;
The other ladies mentioned are not fit
To stand comparison; no, not a bit.
For as the sunlight makes the firelight pall,
My sovereign lady's worth surpasses all,
She is so good, so fair, so welcoming;
May God watch over her in everything.
For, had she not been near to comfort me,
I would have died there, almost certainly,
For fear of Cupid's words and frightful glance,
As I will tell you when I have the chance.

(282–307) Behind the God of Love, upon the green,
Came other ladies numbering nineteen,
Royally dressed, with gentle steps and slow.
After them came more women, row on row,
So many that it startled me to credit
(I would not have believed someone who said it)
That even a third of all that congregation

Had ever lived on earth since the Creation
Of Adam by almighty God above—
And every one of them was true in love.
Now whether this was wondrous, you tell me.
Just at the moment when they first could see
This flower called the daisy, with one motion
They stopped, and knelt before it in devotion,
And sang as with one voice, "Honor to thee,
Our daisy, symbol of fidelity
In women, worthy of the highest praise!
Of this her white crown is the proof always."
And with these words, each lady moved with grace
To sit; they formed a circle in the place.
First sat the God of Love, and then his queen,
She who was crowned in white, and dressed in green;
The others followed suit then and, politely
And in their proper order, sat down lightly.
And not a word was spoken for a while—
About the time it takes to walk a mile.

I, kneeling by this flower, innocent,   (308–335)
Waited to find out what these people meant,
Keeping as still as stone; then, finally,
This God of Love fastened his eyes on me
And said, "Who kneels there?" With the subject broached,
I greeted him respectfully, approached,
And said, "Sir, it is I." "Why are you here?
And to this flower dare you come so near,"
He asked me, "seeing that it is my own?
It were more fitting, if the truth were known,
For something like a worm to draw so nigh."
And I responded, "Sir, may I ask why?"
"Because you have no such ability.
It is my relic, full of dignity
And grace; you are my foe, and speak no good
Of all those who have served me as they should.
Your translating creates disturbances
And hinders folk from their observances
On my behalf. The creed of Love you scorn.
And do not try denying it, I warn:

The Romance of the Rose in your translation
Can now be read without an explanation;
Against my law it is a heresy
Because it makes wise folk withdraw from me.
You wrote of Cressid as seemed good to you;
The story makes all women seem untrue,
Yet they are true as steel can ever be.

(F 335)   Think carefully before you answer me.

(G 268–
316)   Why could you not have said good things as well
As bad ones in those stories that you tell?
Was there no worthy subject in your mind,
Or in your books could you have failed to find
For me some tale of women good and true?
Yes, God knows, sixty books—some old, some new—
You have yourself, with stories worth attention
In which both Greeks and Romans have made mention
Of sundry women, and the lives they had,
Always a hundred good against one bad.
God knows this fact, and so do all the clerks,
Who are accustomed to peruse such works.
What say Valerius, Titus, Claudian?
What says Jerome against Jovinian? [17]
How chaste are maidens, and how true are wives,
How steadfast widows are throughout their lives—
This Jerome tells, nor are their numbers small;
At least a hundred there must be in all;
Reading about them, one feels pain and woe
That for their faith they had to suffer so.

For to their lovers they remained so true
That, sooner than they'd love somebody new,
They chose to end their lives in sundry ways,
And died, as story after story says;
They died by fire, by water, and by blade
Because they would not have their vows betrayed.
At any cost they kept their maidenhood,
Or else their vows as wives or widows good.
They did so not to emulate the saints,

But to be virtuous and free from taints,
And so that men should find in them no flaw;
Yet all the pack lived under heathen law,
These who so dreaded shameful imputations.
So carefully they kept their reputations
That in this world I swear men could not find
A man so able to be true and kind
As was the humblest woman in that day.
And what does Ovid, in the *Epistle*,[18] say
About true wives, the labors they went through?
And Vincent's *Mirror*[19] shows this lesson, too.
By many authors have these things been said,
Christian and heathen, whom you could have read;
You do not have to write the things you do.
What malady could thus be forcing you
To write about the husk and not the corn?
I swear by Venus, of whom I was born,
That although you have followed heresy,
As old fools often do, denying me,
You shall do penance, and it shall be seen!"

Then spoke that noble lady clothed in green,
And said, "My lord, of your munificence,
You ought to listen to this man's defense
Against these accusations you have made.
A god ought not to let himself be swayed.
Your deity should keep a stable mind,
Exerting justice yet remaining kind.
And were you not a god, as all men know,
Then it could come about as I shall show:
This man to you may falsely be accused,
Whereas by right he ought to be excused.
For many tattlers in your court are dwelling,
And many liars, prone to storytelling,
Who serenade you with denunciations
According to their own imaginations.
To seem important, they tell lies to you,
And envy motivates the things they do.
Envy is 'laundress of the court,' or so

(F 341–
361)

Says Dante, for she's certain not to go
From Caesar's house either by night or day;
Whoever else goes, she will always stay.

(362–372)   Also, consider: this man is not smart.
He may have had no wickedness at heart.
It may be he was merely versifying,
Not thinking that his sources may be lying.
Or someone may have told him to compose
Those two works, whom he didn't dare oppose.
Perhaps he has repented by this time.
He has not done so terrible a crime
Translating works of those old, scribbling men
As if he had let malice guide his pen
To make up works himself in Love's despite.

(373–408)   A lord should weigh these things, who would do right,
And not be like the lords of Lombardy,
Who grow rich solely by their tyranny.
He who is lord or king by natural right
Has no need to use cruelty and might.
Though tax collectors bully whom they can,
A king should not mistreat his loyal man,
Who is his treasure and gold in his chest.
Therefore philosophers have found it best
For kings to rule through justice, not through fear;
Their duty in this matter is quite clear.
A king preserves his lords in their degree,
And honors and exalts them suitably;
It is most fitting for a king to prize
Those who are demigods in lesser eyes.
Yet to both rich and poor he should be fair,
Although their earthly states do not compare.
He must take pity on the poor's condition.
Look at the lion's noble disposition!
For if a lion finds a fly annoying,
He acts not like a cur, bent on destroying,
But waves his tail to make the insect flee,
Causing no hurt; for his gentility,

He will not seek revenge on one so slight.
A noble should let mercy temper might,
Considering each thing by equity,
And thinking always of his dignity.
No lord should ever take the right away
Of any man accused to have his say.
This, for a lord, would be an act of shame.
And even if he does deserve the blame,
But asks for mercy with true penitence
And shows himself, forgoing all defense,
To be prepared to suffer your decree,
Then should a god, reflecting prudently,
Weigh his own honor and the mortal's crime.

And, since there is no need for death this time,   (409–441)
You ought to lighten your severity,
Quell anger, and increase benignity.
This man has praised your law and done you good
In writing poetry, as best he could.
Though his poetic talent is quite meager,
Yet he has made untutored people eager
To follow you, in praising of your name.
He wrote the poem called *The House of Fame;*
The Death of Duchess Blanche, [20] an elegy;
The Parliament of Fowls, it seems to me;
Arcite and Palamon [21] are to his credit—
He wrote about their love, though few have read it;
The hymns he's written for your holy days
Include *balades,* roundels, and virelays; [22]
And other holy works worth approbation
Include Boethius in prose translation;
The life of St. Cecelia [23] counts also;
And—although it was done quite long ago—
Origen's *Life of Mary Magdalen.* [24]
He ought to have a lighter penance, then.
His works are great—at least in quantity.
Since you are both a king and deity,
I, your Alceste, [25] who once was queen of Thrace,
Ask for this man, relying on your grace,

That while he lives you harm him in no way.
And he will swear to you, without delay,
Never again in this regard to err,
But tell the kind of stories you prefer,
Of women true in loving all their lives,
Just as you choose, of maidens or of wives,
Thus to promote you, rather than oppose
As he did in *Criseyde* and the *Rose*."

(442–454) The God of Love then answered in this way:
"Madame," he said, "it has been many a day
That I have known you generous and true,
Nor have I found a better one than you
In all this world so far, since the Creation.
If I can do so and preserve my station,
I shall most readily grant your request.
It rests with you, do with him what seems best.
I pardon him, without more dallying.
Whoever would show grace, or give a thing,
And does it promptly, his thanks is the more.
Decide what you will have him do, therefore.
Now thank my lady here," he said to me.

(455–474 I rose, and then sank down upon one knee,
And said this: "Madame, may the God above
Reward you, for you made the God of Love
Forgo his anger with me, and forgive,
And also send me grace so long to live
That I may learn the truth of what you are
Who have so helped and raised me up so far.
Yet, in this case, I truly never meant
To injure love or be malevolent,
Because an honest person, after all,
Shares not in doings of a criminal;
And no true lover should think me to blame
When I expose a fickle one to shame.
In fact, I think they should be laudatory
Because I wrote or told of Cressid's story
And of the Rose; whatever the source meant,

I know this much—that it was my intent
To show that truth in love is to be prized,
While vice and falseness ought to be despised,
By such examples; that was what I meant."

And she replied, "Forgo your argument.   (475–497)
The right and wrong of love can never be
Disputed; and you should learn that from me!
You have the mercy I obtained for you.
Now I shall say what penance you must do
For your trespass; now listen carefully:
You shall, throughout your life, unflaggingly,
Devote the largest portion of your time
To the composing of a glorious rhyme,
A legend of good women, maids and wives,
Those who were true in loving all their lives;
And also tell of men who, false and sly,
Do nothing else for all their lives but try
To see how many women they can shame.
For in your world that now is thought a game.
And though you may choose not to love, firsthand,
Speak well of love; this penance I demand.
And for your sake the God of Love I'll ask
To have his servants help you in your task
And give your labors suitable reward.
Now go your way—this penance is not hard.
The book, when it is done, give to the queen
On my behalf, at Eltham or at Sheen." 26

The God of Love smiled slightly then, and said,   (498–534)
"Do you know whether this is wife or maid,
What rank she is, what honor she is due,
Who has such minor penance given you,
Who have deserved so bitterly to smart?
Pity runs swiftly, though, in gentle heart;
That you may see; she makes known what she is."
"No, as I may be saved," I said to this,
"I do not know more than that she is good."
"There you have said a true thing, by my hood,"

Said Love, "and you may be assured of it,
If only you will stop and think a bit.
Do you not have a book, shut in your chest,
That tells the goodness of the queen Alceste,
She who became a daisy at the end?
She chose to die, her husband to defend
From death, and from hell, where she took his place;
Hercules rescued her, and, by God's grace,
He brought her out of hell to joy again."

"Yes," I said—I had found my answer then,
"I know her now. Is this the good Alceste,
The daisy, and the source of my heart's rest?
Now do I feel the goodness of this wife,
Who has, after her death and in her life,
Both fame and other virtues twice as rare.
She has rewarded fully all the care
I've lavished on the daisy, as her flower.
That Jove has stellified her through his power,
As *Agathon*[27] narrates, is only right.
The emblem of it is her crown of white.
As many virtues make up her renown
As there are tiny flowers in her crown.
For, to immortalize her here on earth,
Cybele made this flower of great worth,
Which wears its own white crown, as all men know.
And Mars gave it a crown of red also,
Instead of rubies, set among the white."

Modesty made her face a little bright
With blushes, when she heard this compliment.
Then Love said, "It was very negligent
Of you not to remember her that time
You wrote 'Hide, Absolon, thy hair' in rhyme;
Her name in it you surely should have set
Because you are so greatly in her debt,
And know so well the good example she
Can set for women who would lovers be.
Of noble love she taught the excellence,

Especially of wifely innocence,
And all the boundaries a wife should keep.
Your meager wits must then have been asleep.
But now I order you, upon your life,
That in your legend you include this wife
With other ladies in your brief narrations.
Farewell; I make no other stipulations.
Before I go, one more thing I should tell—
No faithful lover ever enters hell.

These ladies you see sitting in a row
Appear in your *balade,* as you should know,
And in your books also you can them find.
While writing you should have them too in mind,
At least those of whom you have heard before.
For here are sitting twenty thousand more
Of whom you have not heard, good women all,
And true in love, whatever should befall.
Write about those among them you think best;
I must go home (the sun is sinking west)
To Paradise with all this retinue.
And to the daisy give the honor due.
I wish for Cleopatra to begin
The list; go on from there, my love to win.
Let's see what man could such a lover be
That he would suffer pains as sharp as she.

I know you cannot put all into rhyme
That lovers did and suffered in that time;
It would be over-long to read and hear,
And it suffices for my purpose here
That only the main incidents be told
From those accounts written by authors old.
He who tells many tales must have the sense
To keep them short, or lose his audience."
And with that word, up from my sleep I rose,
And this—my Legend—started to compose.

THE LEGEND OF CLEOPATRA[28]

(580–595)
After the death of Ptolemy the king,
Who had all Egypt in his governing,
Queen Cleopatra governed in that land,
Until it happened that, by Rome's command,
A senator was sent throughout the earth
To conquer kingdoms and increase the worth
Of Rome, as was the custom of that nation,
And so to have the world in subjugation.

This senator, Antonius by name
(Whom Fortune as it happened owed a shame),
Had reached the summit of prosperity
When he grew tired of Rome's authority.
And Caesar's sister, to whom he was wed,
He left—and not a word to her was said—
To take another woman as his wife.
Thus with both Rome and Caesar he had strife.

(596–623)
Nevertheless, authorities agree,
He was a man of great nobility,
And a great loss was suffered when he died.
But passion's ropes had him so tightly tied,
And love had brought him to so sad a state—
His love for Cleopatra was so great—
That the whole world he valued not at all.
All other joy in life began to pall.
To love and serve her was so gratifying,
He had no fear of fighting or of dying
To keep her safe and to maintain her right.

And she, the queen, in turn adored this knight
For his great worth and for his chivalry.
And if books do not lie, then, certainly,
His body and his breeding were so good—
Also his wisdom and his hardihood—
That he ranked with the best in every way.

FIGURE 4. Cleopatra, from a French translation of *De Claris Mulieribus*, early fifteenth century. By permission of The British Library. Royal Fr16.G.v.f.101.

And she was lovely as a rose in May.
And (since to brevity this work aspires)
She married him, and had all her desires.
To write about all the festivity
That then took place, would overburden me,
I have so many stories left to write;
If this took too much space, I'd have to slight
Some subject more pertaining to my charge;
For men may overload a ship or barge.
And therefore, straight to the results I'll skip,
Letting the less important details slip.

(624–649)   Octavian, much angered by this deed,
Gathered an army that he planned to lead
Against Antonius, to conquer him.
With Roman warriors, like lions grim,
He filled his ships—and thus I let him sail.
Antonius knew it, and would not fail
To fight against these Romans if he may.
He made his plans and, on a certain day,
His wife and he and all his regiment
Waited no longer—to the ships they went.
And on the sea it chanced that these foes met.

Trumpeting, shouting, shooting greet the threat;
They steer to get the sun behind their back;
The great gun goes off with a thunder-crack,
And savagely they set to battle sore.
Great stones come hurtling downward with a roar.
The grapnel,[29] full of barbs, grasps where it gropes.
The shearing-hooks[30] run sharp among the ropes.
In with the poleax[31] presses he, and he;
Behind the mast he first begins to flee,
Then out again, and drives him overboard.
He pricks him with the sharp point of his sword;
He rips a sail with hooks as one reaps wheat;
He brings a cup, and cheers them for their feat.
He pours dry peas to trip men if he can.[32]
Pots full of lime[33] man launches against man.

At battle thus the whole long day they spend   (650–668)
Until at last—all things must have an end—
Antonius is beaten, and takes flight,
And all his people flee, who have the might.
The queen flees also, with her purple sail,
From strokes that fall as fast and thick as hail.
It was no wonder that she would not stay.

When Antony saw things turn out that way,
He said, "Alas, the day that I was born!
My honor in this day is turned to scorn."
In desperation, he took up a knife
And pierced his heart with it, to end his life
Before he would go further from the place.
His wife, who could from Caesar have no grace,
To Egypt fled in fear and wretchedness.
Take heed, you men who speak of love's distress,
And falsely threaten dreadful acts you'll do
Unless your mistresses make peace with you;
Observe how women keep the vows they make.

This Cleopatra suffered for his sake   (669–695)
With sorrows such that no tongue could narrate.
But at the dawn she could no longer wait,
And had her skillful craftsmen make a shrine
Of all the rubies and the jewels fine
Of Egypt, that she could find anywhere,
And put in spices to perfume the air,
And had the corpse embalmed; then, at the last,
She had the dead corpse in the shrine sealed fast.
Next to the shrine she had men dig a pit
And drop as many serpents into it
As they could find about them; then she prayed,
"Beloved, whom my heart always obeyed
So fervently from that first blissful hour
When I first swore to put it in your power—
Antonius, my knight, it's you I mean—
That not one waking moment have I seen
When you were absent from my memory

For dance or song, for woe or jollity;
And to myself I made a promise there
That all your feelings, good or bad, I'd share,
As far as it lay in my might to do
(If it were fitting to my wifehood, too);
What you felt, I'd feel also, life or death;
And this same covenant, while I have breath,
I will fulfill; and then this shall be seen:
There never lived and loved a truer queen."

(696–705)   And with that word, naked, this woman brave
Leaped down among the serpents in the grave,
Choosing to make that adders' pit her tomb,
And take their bites upon her as her doom.
This agony and death she meets with cheer
For Antony, who was to her so dear.
This is historical, this is no fable.
Until I find a man so true and stable,
Who will for love his death so freely take,
I pray to God our heads may never ache!

THE LEGEND OF THISBE[34]

In Babylon it happened long ago—   (706–725)
The town Queen Semiramis[35] strengthened so
By having ditches dug, and walls built high
Of hard-baked tiles, the land to fortify—
That there were dwelling in this worthy town
Two noblemen who were of great renown
And lived so close together, on a green,
That just a wall of stone was in between,
Such as one sees in large towns, now as then.

A son was born to one of these two men,
Who grew to be among the bravest there.
The other's daughter was beyond compare
For beauty, in that place and in those days.
And each began to hear the other's praise
From women who were neighbors round about.
For in that country still, without a doubt,
Maidens were kept, out of suspiciousness,
Well-guarded, lest they do some foolishness.
The name of this young man was Pyramus;
The maid was Thisbe—so Ovid tells us.

With both their names so linked in close connection, (726–736)
As they grew older, so grew their affection.
And surely, since their ages merited,
There was no reason that they should not wed
But that their fathers would not give consent.
Both of them suffered love so violent
That friends' attempts to curb it did no good;
But they would meet in private, when they could,
By trickery, and speak of their desire.
Cover the ember, hotter grows the fire—
Forbid a love, it grows ten times as great.

The wall that did these lovers separate   (737–753)
Was cracked from top to bottom, quite in two,

FIGURE 5. Thisbe, from a French translation of *De Claris Mulieribus*, early fifteenth century. By permission of The British Library. Royal Fr16.G.v.f.15.

And had been since the time that it was new.
So narrow was the crevice and so slight
That it was hidden from most people's sight;
But what is it that love cannot espy?
You lovers two, if I am not to lie,
Were first to find this crack, it was so thin.
And softly as one tells a priest his sin,
They spoke to one another through the cleft;
And they would stand and tell, before they left,
All their complaints of love, and all their woe,
As often as they dared arrange it so.
Near to the wall on one side he would stand,
And Thisbe on the other was at hand,
That each the other's whisper could receive—
And thus their guardians they would deceive.

The wall they'd curse and threaten every day   (754–771)
And wish to God that it were torn away;
And they would cry, "Alas, you wicked wall!
Through your envy you will destroy us all.
Why do you not fall down, or break in two?
Or at the least—if you decided to—
You could, just once, allow us both to meet.
If we could once exchange our kisses sweet
We'd have release at last from all our woe.
Nevertheless, some gratitude we owe
Because you have allowed the words we say
Through all your lime and stone to find their way.
For that at least you must be credited."
And when these idle speeches had been said
They both would kiss the chilly wall of stone,
And take their leave, and go their ways alone.
And this was either under twilight's cover
Or very early, lest someone discover.

For a long time they managed matters so;   (772–792)
Till one day, as Phoebus[36] began to glow—
Aurora with her streams of heat had dried
The dew from grasses of the countryside—

Up to this crack, as often was their whim,
Came Pyramus, and Thisbe after him,
And pledged their troth, and swore with all their might
To run away together that same night,
And to deceive their guards so skillfully
That forth out of the city they could flee.
And, since the fields about the town were wide,
So that their time and place would coincide
They settled that their meeting-place should be
Beside King Ninus'[37] tomb, under a tree—
For ancient pagans, idol-worshiping,
In fields at that time did their burying—
And not far from this grave there was a well.
And, that this tale in short space I may tell,
They fixed this covenant without delay;
So long it seemed to them the sun would stay,
That it would never sink beneath the ocean.

This maiden Thisbe had such great devotion,
And such great haste to meet with Pyramus,
That when she saw she might arrange it thus,
At night she stole away in secrecy,
Veiling her head and face concealingly;
To keep her vow, from all the friends she had
She is estranged; alas! it is too bad
That any woman would have been so true
And trusting to a man she hardly knew!
And to the tree she goes with quickened pace—
Love has made her so hardy in this case—
And sits beside the well in readiness.
Alas! then comes a savage lioness
Out of the woods, moving without delay,
Her mouth stained with the blood of recent prey,
To drink out of the well by which she sat.

As soon as Thisbe had caught sight of that,
She rose and, with a heart oppressed by fear
And frightened steps, ran to a cavern near,
Which she could clearly see by the moon's light.

Her veil she let fall from her in her flight;
But she was so afraid, she hardly knew,
And also was so glad for her rescue.
And so she sits in darkness, and keeps still.
And when this lioness had drunk her fill,
Leaving the well, she wandered all around;
Before long the discarded veil she found
And tore in pieces with her bloody jaws.
When this was done, no longer did she pause,
But to the forest once again she passed.

Pyramus to the place has come at last,
But all too long, alas! at home was he.
The moon was shining, he could plainly see,
And on the way, as he came walking fast,
His glances down along the ground he cast.
And in the sand saw, when he looked aside,
The traces of a lion's pawprints wide,
And in his heart he shuddered at the sight,
His face grown pale, his hair on end with fright,
And as he came near, found the dropped veil torn.
"Alas!" he cried, "the day that I was born!
This night the deaths of both lovers will see.
How could I ask that Thisbe pardon me,
When I am he, alas! who did you slay?
My wooing has killed you, this dreadful way.
To bid a woman go by night, alas!
To where some evil thing might come to pass.
And I so slow! How could I fail to be
Here in this place much earlier than she?
Whatever lion roams in this terrain,
Whatever beast, by him I must be slain!
Some creature must devour me in his jaws!"
And with that word he dropped before the gauze
And pressed his lips upon it, sorrowing,
And said, "Alas, veil, now remains no thing
To do, but make you feel my own blood here
As you have felt the blood of Thisbe dear!"
So saying, with a knife he pierced his heart.

(823–852)

The blood out of the wound began to start
Like water from a broken water main.

(853–886) Now Thisbe, who knew nothing of his pain,
Was sitting fearfully, and thinking thus:
"If it should happen that my Pyramus
Came to this place, and me he failed to find,
He may think me deceitful and unkind."
And out she comes, and all around she spies,
Searching both with her heart and with her eyes,
And thinking, "I will tell him of my fear,
The lioness, and all that happened here."

And at the last her lover she has found:
He lies beating his heels upon the ground,
All bloody—back she staggers at the sight,
And like the waves her heart pulses with fright.
As pale as boxtree wood at first she grew,
But soon she thought, and at the last she knew,
That it was Pyramus, whom she loved well.
The deathly look of her now who could tell,
This Thisbe, how she wildly tears her hair,
And how she hurts herself in her despair,
And how she lies upon the ground all still,
And how the tears she weeps his wound do fill,
And how she blends his blood with her complaint;
How with his blood herself begins to paint;
How she embraces his dead body there—
Alas! how does this woeful Thisbe fare!
How she does kiss his frosty mouth so cold!
"Who has done this, and who has been so bold
To slay my love? O speak, my Pyramus!
I am your Thisbe, who calls to you thus!"
And with those words she raises up his head.
This woeful man, not yet completely dead,
When he has heard the name that Thisbe cries,
On her casts up his heavy, deathly eyes,
And down again, and so gives up the ghost.

Thisbe arose with neither noise nor boast (887–899)
And saw the empty sheath, and her veil, too,
And then his sword, with which himself he slew.
Then she spoke thus: "My woeful hand," cried she,
"Is strong enough to do such work for me;
For love shall give me strength and hardiness
To make a wound that's large enough, I guess.
I'll follow you in death, and so shall be
Cause and companion of your death," said she.
"And although nothing less than death, it's true,
Could thus succeed at parting me from you,
Never shall you be parted from me now
More than from death—and I will keep this vow.

"And now, you wretched fathers envious, (900–923)
We who were once your children pray you thus:
To put at last your jealousy aside
That in one grave we may lie side by side,
Since love has brought us to this piteous end.
And righteous God to every lover send,
Who truly loves, more chances to be glad
Than ever Pyramus and Thisbe had!
And let no woman be so confident
As to take part in such an incident.
Yet God forbid but that a woman can
Be just as true in love as any man!
The truth of this shall be made known by me."
With this, his sword she took up suddenly,
Which was still warm with blood her lover shed,
And piercing her heart with it, she fell dead.

And thus are Pyramus and Thisbe through.
Of men faithful in loving I find few
In all my books, except this Pyramus,
And therefore I have spoken of him thus,
For it gives pleasure to us men to find
A man who can in love be true and kind.
However true in love a man may be,
This proves a woman is as good as he.

THE LEGEND OF DIDO[38]

(924–958)

Glory and honor, Vergil Mantuan,[39]
Be to your name! I shall, as best I can,
Follow your guiding lantern as I say
How false Aeneas did Dido betray.
Ovid and the *Aeneid* I will take
As sources, and the main points I will make.

When it had come to pass that Troy must fall
Through Greeks' deceit, and Sinon's[40] most of all,
Who claimed the horse was sent to pacify
Minerva, so that many had to die;
And Hector had, after his death, been seen;
And fire, so fierce that none could intervene,
Was brought to Ilion, that noble tower,
Which all the city trusted for its power;
And the whole city leveled into naught,
And King Priam to utter ruin brought,
Then Venus[41] told Aeneas not to stay;
And so he took Ascanius away,
His little son, whom by the hand he led,
And on his back he carried as they fled
His father, called Anchises, old and gray.
His wife Creusa he lost on the way.
And thus he had much sorrow in his mind
Before his Trojan comrades he could find.
But when they were together at the last,
He was prepared before much time had passed,
And to the sea he hastened with his band,
And set forth quickly, headed for the land
Of Italy, led there by fate's decree.
But to tell his adventures on the sea
Would here be to depart from what I've planned,
And would not suit the subject now in hand.
Of him and Dido, as I said before,
Shall be my tale, and then I say no more.

FIGURE 6. Dido, from a French translation of *Heroides*, ca. 1500. By permission of The British Library. Harley 4867f.51.

(959–
1003)
So long he had to journey on the sea
That at the last to Libya came he
With seven ships, and with no larger band.
And glad he was to hasten to the land,
For he was with the tempest badly shaken.
And when that harbor-refuge he had taken,
A knight, Achates, he chose from the rest,
Finding that one of all of them the best,
To go with him, the countryside to see.
No other would he take for company;
But forth they go, and leave the ships to ride,
His mate and he, with none to serve as guide.

For long they walked through country desolate
Until at last a huntress there they met.
A bow in hand and arrows carried she;
Her clothes were cut off short, above the knee.
She seemed to them to pass, nevertheless,
All Nature's other works in loveliness.
To the two men she called from far away,
Then, coming close, addressed them in this way:
"Have you," she said, "as you have traveled wide
Seen any of my sisters alongside,
With a wild boar, perhaps, or other prey
Which as they hunted might have come their way?
With arrows, and their dresses tucked up so?"
Aeneas answered, "Truly, lady, no;
But by your beauty, so it seems to me,
No earthly woman, surely, can you be,
But Phoebus' sister, worthy of esteem;
And if you are the goddess that you seem,
Have mercy on the woe we have endured."
"I am no goddess," she said, "be assured;
For maidens in this country all dress so,
And go about with arrows and with bow.
The country we are in, Libya we call,
Where Lady Dido is the queen of all."
And briefly all the incidents she told
Through which that region Dido came to hold,

Which at this point I won't put into rhyme;
There is no need—it would be loss of time.
But briefly, it was Venus who that day
Spoke to her son Aeneas in this way.
To Carthage she directed him to go,
Then vanished from them after saying so.
(Though Vergil, word for word, I could pursue,
I fear that it would take too long to do.)

This noble queen named Dido had been wed   (1004–
To Sychaeus, but he had long been dead;   1034)
And she, who was more lovely than the sun,
The noble town of Carthage had begun,
In which with such great honor she held power
That she was thought to be of queens the flower
For beauty, breeding, generosity;
To see her once was thought prosperity;
By kings and lords she was so much desired
That all the world was by her beauty fired;
She stood so high in everyone's opinion.

And thus Aeneas came to her dominion,
And to the greatest of the temples there,
Where Dido at that moment was at prayer.
Aeneas through the town in secret passed,
And when he came into the temple vast
(I cannot say if possible it be),
Venus gave him invisibility—
Without a lie, the book tells it this way.
Aeneas and Achates a survey
Made of the temple, looking all around,
Until a painting on a wall they found
Which the conquest of Troy exhibited.
"Alas, that I was born," Aeneas said.
"Through the whole world our shame has spread so wide
That now it is displayed on every side.
We who were living in prosperity
Are slandered now, to such a great degree
That life to me no longer is worth keeping."

When he had said these words, he started weeping,
So keenly that to see it was a pity.

(1035–
1061)

The noble lady who ruled in that city
Stood in the temple, with royal display,
So richly dressed and fair in every way,
So young, so bright, her eyes so full of mirth
That God himself, he who made heaven and earth,
If he would ever choose a love, for beauty,
Faith, virtue, and regard for woman's duty,
On whom but this lady should his choice fall?
No other is so fit among them all.

Fortune, which has the world in government,
Had brought about a novel incident—
So strange a case has not been seen since then.
For all the remnant of Aeneas' men
Who had been lost at sea, or so he thought,
Not far from that same city had been brought;
And some of them, of greatest excellence,
Had reached the city, by coincidence,
And to the temple come, hoping to meet
The queen, for whose help they would there entreat,
For she was known for her largeheartedness.
And when they had told her all their distress,
The tempest, and the suffering they'd seen,
Aeneas went himself before the queen
And openly made known that it was he.
Who entered then on great festivity—
Who but his men, who'd found their lord and guide?

(1061–
1097)

The queen saw honor done him on each side,
And of Aeneas she had heard before;
And then, it seemed to her, her heart grew sore
That ever such a noble man as he
Should be dishonored to such a degree;
And saw the man, how he was like a knight,
And good enough in person and in might,
And showing promise of nobility,

And able to make speeches pleasingly,
And, as it chanced, having a noble face,
And bones and muscles formed for manly grace—
Venus had given him such handsomeness
That no man could be half so fair, I guess—
And certainly a nobleman seemed he.
And too, because he was a stranger, she
Preferred him, for (by God may we be blessed)
Some find the newest thing to taste the best.

And soon her heart has pity of his woe,
And with that pity, love comes in also;
And thus, for pity and nobility,
He must be rescued from his misery.
She told him, certainly, that she was sad
For all the harm and danger he had had;
And speaking as to one whom she held dear
She said these words, as you may shortly hear:
"Are you not Venus' and Anchises' son?
Truly, all the good things that may be done
To honor and enrich you, I shall do.
Your ships and followers I shall save, too."
And many gentle words to him she spoke,
And also gave instructions to her folk
To go and seek his ships, without delay,
And see them well-supplied in every way.
Much livestock to the ships she had conveyed
And of the wine a lavish present made,
And she herself back to the palace hied,
Keeping Aeneas always at her side.

Need I describe the feast down to the letter?
In all his life, he'd not enjoyed a better,
For all his days were now filled with delights;
Instruments, songs, and revels filled his nights,
And many an amorous glance and sly device.
So has Aeneas come to Paradise
Out of the gulf of hell, and thus in joy
He calls to mind his former state in Troy.

(1098–
1113)

To dancing chambers full of tapestry
And couches rich, arranged with artistry,
Aeneas is led forth after the meat.
There with the queen a while he took his seat;
And when the wine and spices had been passed
Unto his chamber he was led at last,
That he may rest himself and take his ease
With all his folk, to do just as they please.

(1114–
1138)

There was no steed with bridle exquisite,
Nor courser trained and for the jousting fit,
Nor broad-backed palfrey with an easy gait,
Nor bags filled up with gold, heavy in weight,
Nor ornament mounted with jewels bright,
Nor ruby that could by itself give light,
Nor noble falcon that the herons fear,
Nor hound to chase the hart or boar or deer,
Nor goblet of engraved gold, newly wrought,
That in the land of Libya may be bought,
That Dido to Aeneas has not sent—
And all is paid, whatever he has spent.
Her guests may well do honor to this queen,
For one more generous was never seen.

Aeneas to Achates made request
To go to where his vessel was at rest
And fetch his son, and bring back precious things—
A scepter, rich apparel, brooches, rings—
Some for himself to wear, some to present
To her, who had to him such good things sent;
And told his son what ought to be his mien
When he should make these presents to the queen.
Achates comes back, as Aeneas bade;
And he himself is more than ever glad
To see his little son Ascanius.

(1139–
1159)

However—for our author tells it thus—
In the boy's place was Cupid, god of love,
Who at the pleading of Venus above

The likeness of the child agreed to take
So that this noble lady he could make
Enamored of Aeneas; though this may
Be true, I hesitate myself to say.
At any rate, the queen prized him so well,
This boy, that it is wonderful to tell.
And for the presents that his father sent
She thanked him many times, with good intent.
Thus lives the queen in pleasure and in joy
With all these new and lively folk of Troy.
She sought to know all matters that concerned
Aeneas, and from him the story learned
Of Troy, and each of them throughout the day
Would seek the other out to talk and play.
From this began to burn so great a fire—
The foolish Dido now has such desire
To have her guest Aeneas' company—
That she has lost her equanimity.

And now to the result, now to the meat,   (1160–
Why I began this tale, and shall complete—   1187)
Thus I begin: It came to pass one night,
After the moon had raised on high its light,
That this fair queen into her chamber went.
There she began to sigh and to torment
Herself, turning and tossing in her bed
As lovers do—or so I have heard said.
Until at last, she told her sister Anne
About her suffering; thus she began:
"Now, my dear sister, tell me what could be
Making my dreams so terrible," said she.
"This Trojan stranger weighs so on my heart,
For he seems so well-made in every part;
He has such manly virtues, I can tell,
And he can do so many things so well
That all my love, my being, he has won.
Have you not heard him tell all he has done?
Now surely, Anne, if you so counsel me,

I would to him most gladly wedded be.
This is my tale; what good is murmuring?
For life or death, in him lies everything."
Her sister Anne, as one who knows the best,
Replied, and some misgivings she expressed.
She spoke at such length in her sermonizing
That her speech is too long for my reprising.
At last, it did her no good to resist,
For love will love, and it will not desist.

(1188–
1217)

The dawn at last arose over the sea.
The queen, enamored, told her company
To set out nets, and bring spears broad and keen;
For to the hunt will go this lusty queen,
Who is so spurred by this new, happy woe.
All her young folk must to their horses go;
Into the courtyard then the hounds are brought,
And upon steeds that run as swift as thought
Dido's young knights are mounted on each side,
And many women too prepare to ride.
Upon a stalwart palfrey, paper-white,
Its saddle red-embroidered for delight
And set with bars of golden filigree,
Sits Dido, all in gold and jewelry;
She is as lovely as the morning bright
That heals the sick of sorrows felt by night.
Upon a courser skittish as a fire—
A man might guide him with a little wire—
Aeneas sits—a very Phoebus he,
Arrayed with all becoming dignity.
The foamy bridle with the golden bit
He manages just as he wishes it;
And thus I let this noble lady ride
Out hunting, with this Trojan by her side.
The herd of harts before too long is found,
With "Hey! go faster! spur! let go the hound!
Why will the bear or lion not come near,
So that I might once meet him with this spear?"

So say these lusty young folk, as they kill
These wild beasts, which they now have at their will.

During all this, the skies began to lower;　　　　　　　　　(1218–
The thunder rumbled with an awful power;　　　　　　　　　1241)
Down came the rain, with hail and sleet, so fast,
With heaven's fire, that with it was aghast
This noble queen, and all her company,
And each of them was glad enough to flee.
And shortly, from the storm herself to save,
She fled with haste into a little cave.
And at her side Aeneas went also.
If others went with them I do not know;
The author leaves it out of his account.
And in this place the love began to mount
Between them both, for this was the daybreak
Of joy, and the beginning of heartache.
For in that place Aeneas knelt down so,

And told her all his longing and his woe,
And swore to her so deeply to be true,
In good and evil, and not take a new,
And he, like all false lovers, could complain
So well, that Dido, pitying his pain,
Made him her husband and became his wife
Forevermore, as long as they had life.
Together then after the storm was spent,
As they rode out with mirth, so home they went.

The wicked rumor rose without delay　　　　　　　　　　　(1242–
That he had gone alone with her that day　　　　　　　　　1289)
Into the cave; some chose to think it true.
And when King Iarbus[42] of the story knew—
One who had loved this lady all his life
And wooed her, hoping she would be his wife—
So deep the grief was he exhibited
That it is piteous to hear it said.
But love is such that it is often so

That one laughs freely at another's woe.
Aeneas laughs, and is in greater joy
And riches than he ever was in Troy.

O women, innocent and pure of heart,
Mercy, truth, conscience are all on your part.
What could be leading you to trust men so?
Have you such pity on pretended woe,
With old examples thus before your eyes?
Do you not see that all of them told lies?
Where do you see one who did not betray
His love, or hurt her in some other way—
Despoil her, or tell stories of his deed?
And you may see it, just as you may read.
Take heed while of this nobleman I tell,
This Trojan, who knows how to please her well,
Who seems so true and so attentive to her,
So gentle, and so secretive a wooer,
And can so well obedience pretend,
And at a feast or dance on her attend,
And knows so well the methods of romancing,
And waits on her at festivals and dancing,
Rides with her to the temple, or else meets her,
And will not break his fast until he greets her,
And wears heraldic tokens in her honor,
I know not what, and makes up songs upon her,
Jousts, and in arms accomplishes great things,
And sends her letters, tokens, bracelets, rings—
Now, how this lady he will serve, take heed!
Where he had been a point of death from need,
From hunger, from disaster on the sea,
And fleeing his own land in penury,
And far from all his folk by tempest driven,
She has her body and her kingdom given
Into his hand, she who might well have seen
Herself in other lands than Carthage queen,
And lived in joy enough—but why say more?
Aeneas, he who once so deeply swore,

In little time is weary of his play;
His earnest fervor is all blown away.
His ships he secretly prepares for flight,
And makes his plans to steal away by night.

Dido herself suspected some of this,   (1290–
And thought that everything had gone amiss,   1331)
For in his bed he[43] lay at night and sighed.
She asked him why he seemed dissatisfied—
"Why, my dear heart, the one whom I love most?"
"Truly," he said, "tonight my father's ghost
Has in my sleep so sorely me tormented,
And Mercury this message has presented:
That soon, to gain the land of Italy,
I must set sail—it is my destiny.
And for this cause I feel my heart may stop."
With these words, his false tears began to drop
And Dido then close to his side he drew.
"Is that, in truth," she said, "what you will do?
Have you not sworn in marriage me to take?
Of me what kind of woman will you make?
I am a queen, born of nobility—
You will not from your wife thus foully flee?
Alas, that I was born! what shall I do?"

This queen (I briefly tell it now to you)
Beseeches him, begs him to let her be
His slave, his servant lowest in degree;
She falls before his feet—lies swooning there,
In disarray, spreading her bright gold hair,
And says, "Have mercy! let me with you ride!
The lords of all these lands on every side
Will soon destroy me, solely for your sake.
And if you now in marriage will me take,
As you have sworn, I will give you the right
To slay me with your sword this very night!
In spite of all, I should die as your wife.
I am with child—oh, give my child his life!

Have mercy, lord, and pity in your thought!"
But all her agony availed her nought,
For one night, as she slept, he let her lie,
And from her to his band of men did fly,
And at the last set sail, traitorously,
And journeyed to the land of Italy.
And there he wed Lavinia at last,
When Dido into ruin he had cast.

(1332–
1351)
A cloth and sword he left there when he went,
Stealing away from Dido innocent.
Careless, he left them there next to the bed
When to his ships away from her he sped.
When innocent Dido began to wake,
This cloth she pressed with kisses for his sake,
And said, "O cloth, while Jove will it allow,
Unbind me from distress, take my soul now!
Of fortune I have finished all the race."
Alas, thus severed from Aeneas' grace,
Ten times, and twenty, she fell in a faint.
When to her sister Anne she'd made complaint
(The details of this speech I must omit,
So sad it makes me when I write of it),
And told her sister and her nurse to go
To bring back fire and other things also,
Saying she planned a sacrificial rite—
As soon as all seemed ready to her sight,
She leaped upon the pyre that she had made,
And through her heart she drove Aeneas' blade.

(1352–
1367)
But, as my author tells, these words she said
Before she took those steps that left her dead—
She wrote a letter that began this way:
"Like the white swan," she wrote, "which on the day
That it will die then first begins to sing,
I now to you begin my sorrowing.
Not that I hope to get you back again,
For well I know that it is all in vain,

Because the gods are contrary to me.
But since my name is lost through you," said she,
"I may well lose on you a word or letter,
Although I know that I will fare no better;
For that same wind that fills your vessel's sails
Has blown away your promise with its gales."
He who would all this letter have in mind,
Read Ovid,[44] and in him he shall it find.

THE LEGEND OF HYPSIPYLE AND MEDEA

(1368–
1395)

Jason, you root of fickle lovers all,
Cunning devourer, often the downfall
Of gentle women, creatures without guile;
You made a lure and an attractive wile
For ladies of your false nobility
And of your words, flavored with pleasantry,
And of you truthful manner—all pretense—
Your modesty and feigned obedience,
And all your counterfeited pain and trouble.
Most men betray one; you prefer to double!
How many times you swore that love would kill
You, when in fact you never had been ill
Except with lust, which you disguised as love!
If I live long enough, your name I'll shove
Into the English language, and make known
Your sect—so, Jason, now your horn is blown![45]

But certainly, it is a source of woe
That love conspires with fickle lovers so;
For each of them has more prosperity
Than he who suffers for it painfully,
Or who in arms feels many a bloody blow.
The chicken tastes as succulent, we know,
When eaten by the fox who got it free
As by the man who bought it honestly.
Although the farmer owns the fowl by right,
The crafty fox will have his share at night.
With Jason two examples we can see:
The queens Medea and Hypsipyle.

HYPSIPYLE[46]

In Thessaly, according to Guido,[47]   (1396–
  King Peleus was ruling long ago;   1438)
And this king had a brother, called Aeson.
When, in old age, his time was almost done
He gave to Peleus the governing
Of all his land, and made him lord and king.
Aeson had fathered Jason for his heir,
With whom in that day no one could compare
Among the knights for gentleness of birth,
For generosity, and strength, and mirth.
After his father's death he acted so
That there was none who cared to be his foe;
All honored him and sought his company.

King Peleus viewed this suspiciously,
Fearing that Jason thus would mount so high
And such a place of honor occupy
In the regard of nobles in that land
That of his kingdom he would lose command.
And, lying all alone at night, he sought
A way in which destruction could be brought
On Jason, for which he would not be blamed.
And at the last the inspiration came:
Send Jason to some country far away
Where he would surely come to grief some way.
This was his mind, although he made to Jason
Of love and thoughtfulness great demonstration
For fear that those around would spy his thought.
Soon, swift as rumor runs, the news was brought
Of strange events, and the main one was this:
That on an island that was called Colchis
That lay beyond Troy, in the eastern sea,
There was a certain ram, which men might see,
Having a fleece of gold that shone so bright
That nowhere was there any equal sight.
A dragon guarded it both night and day,

FIGURE 7. Hypsipyle, from a French translation of *De Claris Mulieribus*, early fifteenth century. By permission of The British Library. Royal Fr16.G.v.f.19.

And other marvels threatened on the way:
Two bulls, covered with brass instead of hide,
That spit out fire, and yet more had been spied.
The tale would caution anyone who dared
To seek the fleece that he must be prepared
To fight, before attaining his reward,
The bulls and dragon that would be on guard.
And King Aetes lord was of that isle.

King Peleus then hit upon this wile: (1439–
That he his nephew Jason would exhort   1458)
To sail to that land, as a kind of sport;
He told him, "Nephew, if it might come true
That such a noble lot would fall to you
That you this famous treasure might obtain
And to my kingdom bring it home again,
The act would greatly please and honor me,
And bind me to reward you suitably.
And I will pay whatever costs ensue.
Now choose what people you will take with you—
Now we shall see—do you dare take this quest?"
Jason was young, his courage of the best;
He undertook the challenge put to him.
Argus began to put his ships in trim;
With Jason ventured Hercules the strong,
And he chose many more to come along;
If someone asks who undertook the deed,
The Argonauticon[48] he must go read—
It gives a long account, full of details.

Soon Philoctetes had prepared the sails,   (1459–
When they had wind, and brought them speedily   1490)
Out of his native land of Thessaly.
For many days upon the sea they sailed
Until the island of Lemnos they hailed
(All this is not repeated by Guido,
But Ovid, in the *Epistle,* tells it so)
And of this isle the queen and lady was
Hypsipyle, the daughter of Thoas,

The former king; and she was young and fair.
Hypsipyle that day was sporting there
Roaming the cliffs that bordered the seaside;
At once, as it was drawing near, she spied
The ship of Jason coming toward her land.
With good intent, she quickly gave command
To find out whether any stranger might
By tempest have been blown there in the night
To whom she could give aid, as customary,
To help each person and to make him merry
With her great bounty and her courtesy.
The messenger went to them rapidly;
Jason he found and Hercules also,
For they had used a little boat to go
To land, where they could walk and take the air.
The morning was both temperate and fair;
The messenger met with them on the beach
And greeted them with a well-thought-out speech,
Gave them his message, and then sought to know
If they had suffered injury or woe,
Or needed food, or pilot for their aid;
Were they in need, help would not be delayed.
His queen would give whatever they might seek.

(1491–   Jason answered, with words polite and meek:
 1523)   "My lady I must thank with all my heart
For her goodwill; the need is, on our part,
For nothing more than rest from weariness;
If to your beaches we might have access,
When the wind changes, we will go our way."

This lady roamed beside the cliff, at play
With all her company, along the strand.
They came where Jason and the rest did stand
Conversing of these things of which I tell.
This Hercules' and Jason's glances fell

Upon the queen, and to her they made greeting
Hastily and politely at their meeting.
She saw how they behaved and, based upon

Their looks, and words, and clothes that they had on,
Knew they were gentlemen both nobly bred.
And to the castle with her then she led
These strangers, and she entertained them well
And their hardships and labors bid them tell
That they had suffered in the open sea;
So that, within a day, or two, or three,
She'd learned—for his companions told her so—
That it was Jason, whom all men did know,
And Hercules, whose name was praised so high,
For Colchis bound, their strength and skill to try.
Then she paid them more honor than before
And came to spend time with them more and more
For they were worthy people, it was true.
With Hercules she had the most to do;
She trusted him, perceiving him to be
Wise, true, and capable of secrecy;
She sensed no love or yearning on his part,
Or foul suspicions of another's heart.

This Hercules has so this Jason praised
That almost to the sun he has him raised,
Saying that half so true a man in love
Could not be found under the sky above;
Wise, hardy, trustworthy, and rich to boot—
His goodness in these things none could dispute.
In liveliness and in unstinted giving
He far outstripped all others, dead or living;
And then, a noble gentleman was he,
And likely to be king of Thessaly.
He had no flaw, but that he was too meek
To act the lover, and too shy to speak.
For he would rather kill himself, and die,
Than as a lover men should him espy.
"I swear before almighty God I'd give
My blood and flesh (supposing I could live
To see) if only Jason had a wife
Worthy of him; and what a joyous life
The lady could enjoy with such a knight!"

(1524–
1579)

And all of this had been, that very night,
Plotted by Jason and by Hercules.
Those two made up a lie with such great ease
That would rebound upon an innocent!
They fooled the queen by mutual consent.

Jason behaved as coyly as a maid;
His looks were woeful, though no word he said,
But lavishly gave to her counselors
Great gifts, and to her other officers.
Would God I had the leisure and the time
To put the details of his suit in rhyme!
But if in this house a false lover be,
Exactly as he now does, so did he,
In each deceitful trick and subtle deed.
You get no more of me, but you may read
In the original, where all is said.
This is the sum of it—that Jason wed
This queen, and that he took all of her being,
Body and wealth, into his overseeing.
Upon her he begot two children, then
Set sail, and never saw his wife again.
She sent a letter to him, certainly
(Too long to be repeated here by me),
In which she sought his falseness to reprove
And him to pity for her sought to move.
Of his two children she wrote plaintively
That they took after Jason strikingly
Save that they lacked the talent to beguile;
And prayed God that, before too long a while,
She[49] who from her had taken Jason's heart
Would find herself cast in the victim's part
And that her children she would have to kill,
And all of them that let him do his will.
And she was true to Jason all her life,
And kept herself chaste, as befits his wife.
Happiness never reached her heart again,
And she died, for his love, of sorrow's pain.

MEDEA[50]

To Colchis has Duke Jason made his way,   (1580–
Who eats up love as dragons do their prey.   1602)
As matter seeks a form incessantly,
And form to form may pass through easily—
Or as a well can be deep beyond measure—
Just so can this false Jason have no pleasure,
For he is urged on by his appetite
To take of gentlewomen his delight;
In this is all his pleasure and his play.

Jason into the city made his way—
Jaconites its name, the greatest town
Of Colchis, which in that day had renown—
And there the cause of his adventuring
He told to Aetes, that country's king,
And begged him for permission to assay
To bring the golden fleece back, if he may.
The king in turn agreed to his request,
And showed him every honor as a guest,
So much so that his daughter and his heir,
Medea—she who was so wise[51] and fair
That no man ever saw a fairer maid—
To keep this Jason company he made
At dinner, and sit by him in the hall.

Jason was handsome, it is said by all,   (1603–
And like a lord, and very much esteemed,   1628)
And royal as a lion his looks seemed,
His speeches were sincere, and well-rehearsed;
And in love's art and craft he was well-versed;
Without the book, he knew the rules of wooing.
And, because Fortune plotted her undoing,
Medea came to love him desperately.
"Jason," she said, "as far as I can see
Into this matter that you are pursuing,
It well may be the cause of your undoing.

FIGURE 8. Medea, from a French translation of *De Claris Mulieribus*, early fifteenth century. By permission of The British Library. Royal Fr16.G.v.f.20.

FIGURE 9. Medea, from a French translation of *Heroides*, ca. 1500. By permission of The British Library. Harley 4867f.88v.

The man who for the golden fleece will strive
Will not, it seems to me, come back alive
Unless some help from me he might acquire.
But yet," she told him, "it is my desire
To help you to escape calamity
And to return alive to Thessaly."
"My lady," said this Jason in reply,
"That you will feel some sorrow if I die
Or suffer, and that such concern you show,
Neither my might nor labor, as I know,
Can well repay, however long I live.
God give you thanks, beyond what I can give!
I am your man, and humbly I beseech
You for your help—without a longer speech.
Even to death I shall my purpose hold."

(1629–
1650)   At this Medea started to unfold
In every point the dangers of the case,
The battle, and the perils he would face,
Through which no one alive, save only she,
Could help to keep his life in surety.
Then—getting to the point with greatest speed—
Between the two of them they were agreed
That Jason would wed her, as a true knight;
They set a time when he would come at night
Into her chamber, and would promise there
Upon the gods that he, come foul or fair,
Would never any cause for grievance give,
But as her husband all his life would live;
For she had saved him, he owed her this debt.
And not long after this at night they met;
He made his oath, and went with her to bed,
And in the morning on his way he sped,
For she had taught him how he could not fail
To win the fleece, and in the fight prevail.
Thus she saved him from injury and shame,
And also gained for him a victor's name
Through all the tricks of her enchanter's lore.

Now Jason has the fleece; to his own shore
He travels with Medea and her wealth;
Her father does not know; she flees by stealth
To Thessaly, captive of Jason's wooing,
Who yet will be the cause of her undoing.
For at the last to her he is untrue,
He leaves her with their little children two,
And falsely has betrayed all her belief,
As he who was of all love's traitors chief,
And married yet another wife anon,
Who was the daughter of the king Creon.
This is the prize, the honor, and the gain
For all Medea's loving and her pain,
For all her tender heart, her faithfulness,

Who loved him better than herself, I guess,
To leave her father and her legacy.
And this is Jason's great fidelity,
Than whom, in his day, there was never found
A falser lover walking on the ground.
She said this in a letter she composed,
In which his crimes and treasons were exposed:
"Why was I glad your yellow hair to see
More than the limits of my chastity?
Why did I love your youth and handsome face,
And all your pleasing eloquence and grace?
If in your conquest death had taken you,
Great treachery would then have perished too!"
Ovid put well her letter into verse,
Which is too long for me now to rehearse.

(1651–
1679)

THE LEGEND OF LUCRECE[52]

(1680–
1711)

Now must I tell of kings sent to exile
From Rome, because their actions were so vile,
And of the last king, called Tarquinius,
As Ovid says, and Titus Livius.[53]
But not for that cause do I tell this story,
But for the praise and the remembered glory
Of that true wife Lucrece, whose faithfulness
To vows of wifehood and great steadfastness
Won praise not just from pagans for her deed
But also from the one called in our creed
Augustine; he too spoke with great compassion
About Lucrece, who perished in this fashion.
Of how she died, the details I will spare
And only the main points will I declare.

When at the seige of Ardea had been
For many days the mighty Roman men
Without achieving many deeds of worth,
Their idleness was turned to thoughts of mirth;
And in his play, Tarquinius the young
Began to joke, for he was quick of tongue,
And said it was indeed an idle life;
No man among them did more than his wife.
"Let us now speak of wives—that is my whim—
Each man shall praise his, as she seems to him,
And let us ease our spirits with the game."
One knight spoke—Collatinus was his name—
And said thus: "No, sir, for there is no need
To trust in words, but rather in the deed.
I have a wife," he told him, "who, I swear,
Is said by all to be beyond compare.
Let us return to Rome tonight and see."
Tarquinius replied, "That pleases me."

(1712–
1744)

So back to Rome they hasten with great speed;
To Collatinus' dwelling they proceed,

FIGURE 10. Lucrece, from a French translation of *De Claris Mulieribus*, early fifteenth century. By permission of The British Library.

Tarquinius and Collatinus too.
The husband of a hidden entrance knew,
So that the house they entered secretly,
No porter stationed by the gate to see,
And to the chamber door the two men sped.
This noble wife was sitting by her bed,
Thinking no ill, in casual array,
And working with soft wool, as our books say,
To keep herself from sloth and idle hands.
And for her servants' work she gave commands,
And asked of them, "What tidings do you know?
What say men of the siege? How does it go?
Would it were God's will that the walls fell down!
My husband has been too long out of town.
Because of this my dread is so severe
It pierces through my heart as would a spear
When I think of the siege or of that place.
God save my lord, I pray him through his grace!"

And having said these mournful words, she wept,
And of her work no further heed she kept,
But looked down modestly, to hide her feeling—
And that expression made her most appealing.
And her tears also, full of probity,
Increased her look of wifely chastity;
Thus does her face seem worthy of her heart—
In deed and show each takes the other's part.
Her husband Collatinus, listening there,
Went rushing in before she was aware
And said, "Fear nothing—I am in this place!"
And she rose quickly, with a joyful face,
And kissed him, as by wives is often done.

(1745–   Tarquinius, the arrogant king's son,
1774)   Took notice of her beauty and expression,
         Her yellow hair, her shape, and her discretion,
         Her face, her words, the theme of her complaint
         (And that her beauty did not come from paint)
         And he was taken by such great desire

For her that his heart burned him like a fire
So madly that his wits were all undone;
For well he knew that she could not be won;
Ever the more he felt himself despair,
The more he wanted her and thought her fair.
His blind desire was all his coveting.

The next day, when the birds began to sing,
He rode back to the siege, to all unknown,
And sorrowfully he walked about alone
Wishing his image of her to renew:
"Her hair fell in this way; this was her hue;
This way she sat, spoke, spun; this was her face;
This was her beauty, and this was her grace."
This fancy has his heart so quickly taken,
And as the sea with tempests is so shaken
That even when the storm has passed away,
The water is still troubled for a day,
Just so, although her form itself is gone,
The pleasure it affords him lingers on;
Not pleasure, even so, but foul delight,
Or an unrighteous, hateful appetite—
"Despite herself, my lover she shall be!
Chance comes to help the brave man out," said he.
"Whatever comes of it, let it be so."

He girded on his sword, prepared to go,
And forth he rode until he came to Rome,
And made his way until he reached the home
Of Collatinus, where he was before.
The sun had set, and it was night once more.
He came into the house a secret way
And like a thief by night he sought his prey
When everyone had gone to take his rest
And fear of treason troubled no one's breast.
By window, or by other trickery,
With ready sword he came in speedily
To where the noble wife Lucretia slept.
She wakened as into her bed he crept.

(1775–
1811)

"What beast is that," she said, "that presses thus?"
"The king's own son am I, Tarquinius,"
He said, "and if the slightest sound you make,
Or if a creature here should chance to wake,
By God I swear to you, before I part,
That with this sword I'll stab you to the heart."
With this, he seized her, and her throat he caught,
And the sword's point against her heart he brought.

No word she spoke—such strength she could not find—
What could she say? Confounded is her mind.
Just as a wolf that finds a lamb alone,
To whom can she complain, or make a moan?
What! shall she struggle with a hardy knight?
Well do men know a woman has no might.
Shall she cry out, or find escape by art
From him who holds her throat, sword to her heart?
Mercy she begs, and says all that she can.
"So you will not," replies this cruel man,
"Or else, as Jupiter my soul may save,
There in your stable I shall kill your slave
And lay him in your bed, and swear it true
That in adultery I discovered you.
And thus will you be dead, and also lose
Your name; another way you cannot choose."

(1812–
1853)

These Roman wives so dearly loved their name
During that time, and so much dreaded shame,
That, what with fear of slander and of death,
She lost her wits together with her breath,
And in a swoon she lay, and seemed so dead
That men may cut her arm off, or her head;
She can feel nothing, either foul or fair.
Tarquinius, who is a royal heir,
And should, as well by lineage as by right,
Acquit himself as does a lord and knight,
Why have you done offense to chivalry?
Why have you done to her this villainy?
Alas! that you have done a villain's deed!

But to the purpose: in the tale I read
That when he'd gone, after this crime occurred,
To all her friends the lady then sent word—
Her father, mother, husband, all she knew—
And with disheveled tresses, bright of hue,
And dressed as women those days would be dressed
To go to see a dear friend laid to rest,
She takes her seat beside them, sighing low.
Her friends inquire what illness plagues her so,
And who is dead; and she sits weeping still;
For shame she can say nothing, good or ill,
Nor yet to meet their gazes is she bold.
But at the last the story she has told
Of Tarquin's deed and of her sad disgrace.
No one could tell the sorrow in that place
That she and all her friends together felt.

Even a heart of stone would surely melt—
And its possessor would feel sorry, too—
So wifely was this woman's heart, and true.
She said that, for her guilt and for her blame,
Her husband would not have a filthy name—
She would not, come what may, let that befall.
And then they answered and assured her, all,
That they forgave her, as was only right.
There was no guilt—it lay not in her might—
And told her of examples from the past.
But it was all for nought; she said at last,
"Of this forgiveness much ado you make;
Forgiveness is a gift I will not take."

And then, unseen by all, she drew a knife
And with its blade she ended there her life;
And yet she looked, as she was falling down,
And heeded the arrangement of her gown;
For even in her dying she took care
So that her feet and all would not lie bare,
So well she loved her cleanness and her vows.
All those in Rome did then her cause espouse;

(1854–
1885)

Brutus by her chaste blood an oath did take
That Tarquin should be banished for her sake,
And all his kin; he called to him the folk;
Before them of the dreadful deed he spoke,
And had her carried forth upon a bier
Through all the town, that men might see and hear
The horror of Lucretia's ravishing.
Never again did Romans have a king
After that day; and she was thought to be
A saint, and her day held in sanctity
By Roman law; and so this noble wife,
As Titus has borne witness, ends her life.

I tell it, for she was of love so true,
Nor in her will did she change for a new;
And for the stable heart, earnest and kind,
That in these women men may always find.
For where they cast their heart, there it will stay.
And well I know that Christ himself did say
That in the land of Israel nowhere
Did he find faith so great as to compare
With that of woman; and this is no lie.
But as for men, what evil one can spy
In all their acts! Assay them if you must;
The truest is a fragile thing to trust.

THE LEGEND OF ARIADNE[54]

Minos, infernal judge, of Crete the king,   (1886–
Your lot is drawn, now come you in the ring.   1927)
Not just for you I write this history,
But also to recall to memory
The great deceit of Theseus in love;
For which the very gods in heaven above
Were angry, and took vengeance on your sin.
Be red for shame! your life I now begin.

Minos, Crete's mighty ruler in his day,
Who had a hundred cities in his sway,
To Athens sent Androgeos, his heir,
To learn philosophy; it turned out there
That he was put to death in that same town
By persons envious of his renown.
Minos, the mighty king of whom I speak,
Fit vengeance for his son has come to seek.
Alcathoe besieged he hard and long;
Nevertheless, the walls there were so strong,
And its King Nisus was a knight so great
That little did he fear the city's fate.
For Minos' plotting he felt scant concern
Until fate took an unexpected turn.
For Nisus' daughter on the battlement[55]
Stood looking out to see how the siege went,
And it so chanced that, as she stood above
And saw King Minos fight, she fell in love
With his chivalric ways and handsomeness,
And sorely feared to die from her distress.
To finish quickly what we have begun,
She made things turn out so that Minos won
The city, and could have it at his will,
To rescue whom he pleased, or else to kill.
He returned evil for her kindliness,
And would have let her drown in her distress,
Had not the gods pitied here misery;

FIGURE 11. Ariadne, from a French translation of *Heroides*, ca. 1500. By permission of The British Library. Harley 4867f.74v.

But all that tale is now too long for me.
And so Alcathoe to Minos fell,
Then Athens, and then other towns as well,
With this result: that Minos has so driven
The men of Athens, that he must be given
From year to year some of their children dear
To be a sacrifice, as you shall hear.

Minos a monster[56] had, an evil beast,
Which on the flesh of living men would feast;
So strong it was that it could not be beaten
And no man could escape from being eaten.
And so, as every third year came about,
They cast lots and, however it fell out,
Rich man or poor, his son he had to take
And of the child a present had to make
To Minos, who would choose to save or kill,
Or let his beast devour him at its will.
This is what Minos chose to do for spite;
Avenging his son's death gave him delight,
And making those of Athens serve his whim
From year to year, while life was left to him.
He left the town subdued, and home he sailed.

(1928– 1942)

This custom had for many years prevailed
Until at last Egeus, Athens' king,
His own son Theseus was forced to bring—
Since upon him has fallen now the lot—
To be devoured; and mercy there is not.
So forth is led this young knight, sorrowing,
Into the palace of Minos the king,
And into prison, fettered, cast is he
Until the time when eaten he should be.
Well may you weep, O woeful Theseus,
Who are a king's son and imprisoned thus!
It seems that you would owe a sacred debt
To anyone who saved you from this threat;
And if a woman came to rescue you,
You ought then to become her servant true
And as her lover ever after dwell.

(1943– 1958)

(1959–
1984)
But to return now to the tale I tell:
The place where Theseus bemoaned his plight
Was a deep dungeon, far from the sunlight,
And separated, by a wall between,
From where the princesses had their latrine.
They lived in roomy chambers overhead—
Which fronted on the largest street that led
Through Athens—in great joy and affluence.
It happened, by some odd coincidence,
When Theseus by night was sorrowing,
That Ariadne, daughter of the king,
And Phaedra, too, her sister, heard it all—
His every word—as they stood on the wall
Where they had gone to gaze upon the moon.
They did not wish to go to bed so soon;
And they were moved to pity by his woe.
For a king's son to be imprisoned so,
And be devoured, seemed to them a great shame.
This Ariadne called her sister's name
And said to her, "My lovely sister dear,
This woeful nobleman can you not hear,
How pitifully he mourns for all his kin,
And also for the state he now is in,
And guiltless? He has reason to lament.
And, by my honor, if you will consent,
He shall be helped, whatever else we do."

(1985–
2024)
"Yes," answered Phaedra, "I feel sorry, too,
As much as I have felt for any man.
And if we are to help him, our best plan
Is to command the jailer secretly
To come in haste and speak with you and me,
And also bring this woeful man along.
If he can overcome the monster strong,
Then he will win; there is no other way;
The bottom of his heart we must assay—
Were he to have a weapon well-concealed,
Would he then dare, his life to keep and shield,
To fight the monster, and himself defend?

For in the prison where he must descend,
As you well know, the beast is in a place
That is not dark, and has sufficient space
To wield an ax or sword or staff or knife.
So he, it seems to me, could save his life,
And if he is a man, he will do so.
And we shall make for him some balls also
Of wax and tow; and when it opens wide

Its mouth, then he can throw the balls inside
To dull its hunger and obstruct its bite.
When Theseus decides the time is right
To brave the choking beast, he shall attack
To kill before it gets its power back.
This weapon shall the jailer hide away
Inside the prison long before that day.
But then, the house is crisscrossed to and fro
With cunning passages by which to go—
Just as the maze is shaped, it is designed;
For this I have a remedy in mind;
A clew of twine, unwinding as he goes,
Will lead him back the same way, I suppose,
If he is careful to keep it in sight.
When he has overcome the creature's might,
Then he may flee from all this dread and woe,
And help the jailer to escape also,
And in his own land find prosperity,
Since such a powerful lord's son is he.
This counsel, if he dares, he ought to take."

Why should I now a longer story make?
The jailer comes, and with him Theseus.
And when these matters have been ordered thus,
Then Theseus gets down upon his knee:
"The rightful lady of my life," said he,
"I, woeful man, condemned to certain death,
From you, as long as I have life and breath,
When this is past, myself I will not sever,
But in your service will remain forever

(2025–
2053)

As a poor man unknown to anyone,
And serve you thus until my life is done.
I shall renounce my wealthy family
To be in court your page, of low degree,
Provided you assure me in this place
That at that time you'll give me, of your grace,
Enough to eat and drink—no more. And, too,
I'll do whatever work you bid me do,
That Minos and his men, who never yet
Have seen me, would not know me if we met.
I'm certain that I will not be espied,
So cleverly my features I shall hide.
A servant's humble bearing will disguise me
So that no man alive will recognize me—
To save my life, and have the company
Of you who have so kindly treated me.
Upon my father too I shall prevail
To help this man, the keeper of your jail,
And honor him so well that he shall stand
Among the greatest nobles in my land.

(2054–
2073)
"And if I dared to say it, lady bright,
I am a king's son, and also a knight.
I wish to God, if it might happen so,
That all of you to my own land could go
And I also, to bear you company;
You would see if I speak deceptively.
And when, in lowly state, I offer you
My service as a page, humble and true,
Then if I do not serve you in that place
I pray to Mars to grant me, by his grace,
That shameful death upon me may descend
And death or poverty on every friend,
And that my spirit in the night may go,
After my death, and wander to and fro,
Wearing eternally a traitor's name
To trouble my soul's rest, and do me shame!
And if I claim a lordlier degree,
Other than one you may bestow on me,

May I die shamed, just as I said before;
And mercy, lady—I can say no more."

Theseus was a handsome knight to see,   (2074–
And young, for he was only twenty-three.   2102)
But anyone who saw him looking so,
And heard him speaking, might have wept for woe.
And Ariadne, framing her replies,
Responded to his words and to his eyes: [57]
"A king's son, and also a knight," said she,
"To be a servant in such low degree,
May God forbid, lest it shame women all,
And grant that such a thing never befall!
But send you grace of heart, and craft also,
To save yourself, and bravely slay your foe!
And grant that after this I may you find
To me and to my sister here so kind
That I do not repent saving your life!
Yet were it better that I were your wife,
Since you are in nobility my peer

And have a kingdom too, not far from here,
Than that I let you perish, innocent,
Or to your labor as my page consent.
The offer does not suit your rank, it's true—
But pressed by fear, what will a man not do?
As to my sister, seeing it is so
That she must come with me, if I should go,
Or suffer death such as would fall to me,
A proper wedding you must guarantee
For her to your son, at your homecoming.
This is the end of all my bargaining;
Now swear to it on all that may be sworn."

"Yes, lady," said he, "or may I be torn   (2103–
To pieces by the Minotaur so fierce.   2135)
And further to affirm it, you may pierce
My veins, and draw blood, as a pledge to you;
Had I a knife or spear, this I would do,

And swear by it, and so your fears relieve.
By Mars, in whose great power I believe,
If it should happen that I live and win
The battle that I soon must enter in,
From this place and from you I would not flee
Until the proof of my words you would see.
For if the truth to you I were to tell,
I long have loved you, faithfully and well,
In my own country, though you did not know,
And most desired the sight of you also
Above all other creatures anywhere.
Upon my honor, then, to you I swear
That seven years I've served you faithfully.
Now I have you, and you also have me,
My dearest one, of Athens the duchess!"

She smiled with pleasure at his steadfastness
And at his heartfelt words, and face sincere,
And to her sister spoke as you shall hear:
"Now, sister mine," she said, her voice pitched low,
"A duchess I shall be, and you also,
And joined to the blood royal by such means
That both of us are likely to be queens;
A king's son it is well that we should save,
For so a gentlewoman should behave
Toward one of royal blood, given her might,
In a good cause—that is, his lordly right.
Upon us for this deed there lies no blame,
Nor should we have for it an evil name."

(2136–
2162)

To tell the story in the shortest way,
Theseus took his leave; then, the next day,
Every detail was carried out in deed
As in the covenant they had agreed.
His weapon, clew, and all that I have told
The jailer carried into the household
To that place where the Minotaur would wait
Theseus' coming, right beside the gate.
And Theseus unto his death is led,
And forth to meet the Minotaur is sped;

And, fighting it according to instruction,
He overcomes and brings the beast's destruction,
And out again he by the clew is led
In secrecy, after the beast is dead;
And by the jailer he procures a barge
And fills it up with his wife's treasure large
And takes his wife, and Phaedra, and also
The jailer—all who helped to overthrow
The monster, and they flee that land by night
And thence to Oenopia they take flight
Where friends would help them in their journeying.
There they have banquets, there they dance and sing;
And he has Ariadne in his arms,
She who has kept him safe from many harms.
He is presented with a barge all new
And treasure by his countrymen there, too,
And takes his leave, and makes his way toward home.

And at an island, circled by sea-foam,   (2163–
On which to live no earthly creature chose   2196)
Except wild beasts—and there were lots of those—
He made his ship to come along the shore,
And left it there for half a day or more,
And said that he would take his ease on land.
His mariners all heeded his command;
And not to make of it a longer story,
While his wife slept there on the promontory,
Because her sister was more fair than she,
He took her by the hand, and forth went he
To ship, and as a traitor stole away
While Ariadne in deep slumber lay,
And homeward to his country he sailed fast—
To twenty devils may the wind him cast!
And found his father dead, drowned in the sea.
But more of him you will not get of me:
These lovers false by poison should be slain!

Of Ariadne now to speak again,
Who, in her weariness, with sleep was taken,
In sorrowing her heart may now awaken.

Alas! for you my heart with pity aches!
That morning, just at dawn, as she awakes
She feels the bed, and finds herself forlorn.
"Alas!" she said, "that ever I was born!
I am betrayed!" she cried, and tore her hair,
And ran down to the shore, her feet all bare,
And cried out, "Theseus! my lover dear!
Where are you, that I do not find you here,
And may be slain by some wild beast's attack?"
Only the hollow hills made answer back.
Seeing no man—the moon some brightness cast—
High up onto a rock she went at last,
And saw his barge sail from her, out to sea.

(2197–
2227)
At this her heart grew cold, and thus said she:
"Kinder than you I find these creatures wild!"
Had he not sinned, who had her thus beguiled?
She cried, "Turn back—for shame and fear of sin—
Your barge! All of its travelers are not in!"
Her kerchief on a pole she set on high
Hoping that it might chance to catch his eye,
Reminding him that she was left behind,
So he would turn, and on the shore her find.
For nothing—he is gone—she is alone.
Then, swooning, she sank down upon a stone—
And up she rose, and kissed with tender care
The footprints he had left when walking there,
And turning to her bed, lamented thus:
"You bed, who used to welcome two of us,
For two, not one, you took your solemn vow!
Where has the greater part of you gone now?
Exiled, what shall become of me, alas!
For even if some ship or boat should pass,
Home to my land I dare not go, for fear.
No counsel can I find to give me cheer."

Why should I tell of her complaining more?
The length of it would make it quite a chore,
And Ovid tells it in another place;

But I shall tell the end in a short space.
The gods have helped her, for their charity,
And in the sign of Taurus men may see
The jewels of her crown,[58] down to this day.
Nothing more of this matter will I say;
But any lover who, as I record,
Would dupe his love—the devil him reward!

THE LEGEND OF PHILOMELA[59]

(2228–
2256)

You giver of all forms, you who have wrought
This world so fair, and bore it in your thought
Eternally, before your work began,
Why did you make, to be a shame to man,
Or—although it was not your purposing
To gain that end, by making such a thing—
Why let a man like Tereus be born,
Who is in love so false and so forsworn
That from this world up to the highest sphere
The foulness spreads, when people name him here?
And as for me, so grisly was his deed
That when the foul tale of the man I read
My very eyes grow foul and sore also.
Still lasts the venom of so long ago,
Infecting whosoever will behold
The story of this man of whom I told.

Of Thrace he was the lord, and kin to Mars,
The god whose bloody sword betokens wars;
And he was wed, with great festivity,
To King Pandion's daughter, fair to see.
She was called Procne, flower of her land;
Though at the feast Juno was not at hand,
Nor Hymen, who is god of marrying,
Yet to the feast, their torches carrying,
Came the three Furies, harbingers of blight.
The owl flew round about the eaves all night,
Prophet of misery and of mischance.
This celebration, filled with song and dance,
Lasted a fortnight, give or take a day.

(2257–
2287)

To end this story in the shortest way—
I tire of him whose tale I have begun—
Five years his wife and he had lived as one,
When she began upon a day to grieve,
Missing the sister she had had to leave,

So sharply that she knew no words to say.
But still her husband she began to pray,
As he loved God, to grant her this one boon—
To see her sister, and return home soon;
Or if his choice was that her sister be
The one to come, to fetch her speedily.
And this was, day by day, her constant prayer,
In humble words expressed with wifely care.
This Tereus prepared his ships at last,
And to the land of Greece his way has cast.
There his wife's father he began to pray
That a month's visit he would not gainsay
For Philomela, that she might once more
Be with her sister Procne as before—
"And she will come back to you speedily,
For I myself shall bear her company;
Just as my own heart's life, her life I'll keep."
Pandion the old king began to weep,
And greatly did he, tenderhearted, grieve
To miss his daughter, and to let her leave.
In all the world he treasured nothing so;
But finally he gave her leave to go.
For Philomela, salt tears on her face,
Was eager to beseech her father's grace
That she should go to see her sister dear;
And in her arms she held her father near.

In all she did she seemed so young and fair   (2288–
That Tereus, seeing her beauty rare—   2307)
No other woman was so finely dressed,
And yet in beauty was she twice as blessed—
Has cast his heart on her, without recall:
He must have her, whatever may befall.
He knelt and pleaded, using every wile,
Until Pandion said, after a while,
"Now, son," said he, "who are to me so dear,
To you I will entrust my daughter here,
Who bears with her the key of my heart's life.
Greet now for me my daughter and your wife,

And give her leave to come here, so that I
May see her once again before I die."
And then he had prepared a lavish feast
For him, and for all those, greatest and least,
Who came with him, and gave him treasure, too,
And he himself accompanied him through
The streets of Athens, till they reached the sea,
And then turned home; of no ill will thought he.

(2308–
2329)
With oars the vessel makes its journey fast,
And at the shores of Thrace arrives at last;
Into a forest then he made her go,
And took her to a cave where none would know.
And in this cave—if she liked his request
Or liked it not—he ordered her to rest;
For which her heart quaked, and she asked him thus—
"Where is my sister, brother Tereus?"
And with these words she wept, a woeful sight,
And, pale and pitiful, trembled with fright,
Just as the lamb does which the wolf has bitten,
Or as the dove does, by the eagle smitten,
Which from its claws a safe escape has made
And yet is still bewildered and afraid
Lest it be caught; she sat like such a thing.
Yet from this there will be no rescuing.
The thief has used such force on her that he
At last has taken her virginity
Despite her wishes, by his strength and might.
Behold a man's deed, in the cause of right!
"Sister!" she cries aloud, and "father dear!"
And "God in Heaven, give help to me here!"

(2330–
2347)
She cries to no avail; and her false brother
Has added to this outrage yet another.
Fearing lest she make known to all his shame,
And give him among men a villain's name,
From her mouth with his sword her tongue he cuts,
And her forever in a castle shuts,
Where she must dwell in prison, a recluse,
Where she will have to serve his lustful use,

Nevermore from this bondage to depart.
Sad Philomela, woeful is your heart!
May God avenge you, and your prayers avail!
Now is it time for me to end this tale.
When Tereus rejoined his wife at last
He took her in his arms, his face downcast,
And piteously wept, and shook his head,
And told her he had found her sister dead;
Innocent Procne thought her heart would break,
Such grief she suffered for her sister's sake.

And thus in weeping I let Procne dwell,   (2348–
And more about her sister I will tell.   2372)
This woman pitiful once, long ago,
Had learned how to embroider and to sew,
And also how to weave a tapestry,
A skill well known to women formerly;
And truly she was left with a supply
Of meat and drink and clothing all nearby.
Though both to read and copy she was taught,
Yet with a pen she could not write her thought.
But she could weave the letters one by one,
And in this way, before the year was done,
She wove a piece of woolen fabric large
Telling how she was brought there on a barge,
And forced inside the cave, where she was still;
And how this Tereus had done his will
She clearly wove, and wrote the text above
Of how she suffered for her sister's love.
All that had happened she told to a slave
By signs, and then to him her ring she gave
And sent him to the queen, the cloth to take.
She told him, with the signs that she could make,
That she would give him what reward she could.
He hurried to the queen, this servant good,
And took the cloth, and told all that had passed.

When Procne had her eyes upon it cast,   (2373–
No word, for grief and anger, did she say   2393)
But feigned a pilgrimage on the next day

To Bacchus' temple; in a little while
Her dumb sister she found in prison vile,
Sitting and weeping softly, all alone.
Alas! for many a complaint and moan
Does Procne pour out on her sister's harms.
Each of them takes the other in her arms,
And thus I let them in their sorrow dwell.

The remnant is not burdensome to tell,
For this is all of it: thus was she served
Who'd done no evil and had not deserved,
That she knew of, harm from this cruel man.
Think of this, and beware men if you can.
For even though he may not act, for shame,
Like Tereus, lest he lose his good name,
Nor serve you as a murderer would do,
Yet not for very long will he be true—
And I would say this, though he were my brother—
Unless he fails to get himself another.

THE LEGEND OF PHYLLIS[60]

By proof as well as by authority,   (2394–
   That wicked fruit comes from a wicked tree   2451)
You may find out, if you would like to know.
But it is for this end that I speak so:
To tell Demophoön's great villainy.
I've heard of none more false in love than he,
Unless it was his father Theseus.
"From such a lover, Lord, deliver us!"
So women pray who hear of such a one.
Now it is time my story were begun.

When Troy had been defeated utterly
Demophoön set sail upon the sea
Toward Athens, where he had a palace grand.
With him came many ships and barges manned
By countrymen of his, and many lay
Wounded and sick, in sorrow and dismay,
From fighting so long on a foreign shore.
Behind them came a wind and a downpour
That drove so hard, his sail could not withstand
And more than all the world, he wished to land,
Thus hunted by the tempest to and fro.
It was too dark, he found no place to go;
Waves broke the helm, so that he could not guide
The ship, which was so battered on each side
That carpenters could never put it right.
The sea was burning like a torch at night,
Madly, and tossing him first up, then down,
Till Neptune had compassion, lest he drown,
With Thetis, Caurus, Triton, and the rest,
Who saw to it that on land he was pressed
To where Lygurges' daughter was the queen;
Phyllis her name was, fairer to be seen
Than is the flower in the shining sun.
Almost too late the rescuing is done;
Demophoön is weak, his people worn

FIGURE 12. Phyllis, from a French translation of *Heroides*, late fifteenth or early sixteenth century. By permission of the Master and Fellows of Balliol College.

With hardship, and by famine also torn
So that to death they had been nearly driven.
His wise folk to him have this counsel given:
That from the queen he should seek remedy,

And also find out what his chance may be
Of finding in her kingdom some relief
From all their wants, and comfort for their grief.
For he was sick, and very near to death;
He'd scarcely strength to speak or draw his breath,
And in Rhodope stayed and sought to rest.
When he could walk again, he thought it best
To make his way to court and there seek aid.
Men knew him, and great honor he was paid
As duke and lord of Athens, nobly born—
Titles his father Theseus had worn,
Who in his time enjoyed so great a name
That no man in the region had more fame.
He was like Theseus in looks and height,
And false in love—all this was his birthright.
As does Reynard the fox, the fox's son,
He knew the tricks his father once had done
By instinct, not by lore, as ducks can swim
When they are caught and carried to the brim.[61]

Phyllis meets him and puts him at his ease;
His looks and speech are able her to please.
But, as it sickens me to write this way
About those who their faithful loves betray,
And as I would speed up my legend's pace
(To bring it to a close God send me grace!),
I will tell it as briefly as I can.
You've heard already Theseus' foul plan
For tricking Ariadne, Minos' daughter,
Who in her pity rescued him from slaughter.
Briefly, Demophoön in his own day
Likewise directed his steps in the way
Taken by his false father Theseus.
Therefore to Phyllis he has promised thus

(2452–
2486)

To wed her, and has sworn by all things good,
And then has stolen everything he could
When he is rested and no longer ill;
And also he has Phyllis at his will,
As I could easily, if I wished to,
Have told all that took place between the two.

He said he must go home for a short stay
To bring back garments for their wedding day
Befitting her high rank, and his also.
Quite openly he took his leave to go
And told her that he would not long remain,
But in a month's time would return again;
He gave commands as if he were in fact
Lord of that land, and took all that he lacked
With kindly thanks; and had his ships restored
As quickly as he could, and got on board.
But unto Phyllis he came not again;
And his deceitfulness caused her such pain
Alas! that, as the histories record,
At last she took her own life with a cord
When she was sure that she had been betrayed.

(2487–
2517)
But first she wrote Demophoön and prayed
That he would come and rescue her from grief.
I'll tell a word or two, but I'll be brief.
Of him I choose not very much to think
Or to expend more than a little ink
For he was false in love, as was his sire.
The devil set both of their souls on fire!
But still of Phyllis' letter I will write
A word or two, although it will be slight.
"Your hostess, once, Demophoön," said she,
"Your Phyllis, who now feels such misery,
She of Rhodope, must complain to you
Over the date agreed on by us two,
That you do not hold to it, as you said.
Your anchor, which you in our harbor laid,
Promised us you would come, without a doubt,

Before one cycle of the moon was out.
But four times has the moon now veiled her face
Since that day when your ships sailed from this place,
And four times has she lit the world anew.
Despite this—I speak only what is true—
As yet the stream of Sytho has not carried
Your ship from Athens, that we may be married.
If you would call to mind when you were due
As I, or any would whose love was true—
You'd find I don't complain ahead of time."
All that she wrote I may not put in rhyme,
For to do so would surely try my strength,
The letter being of so great a length.
But into verse I put, at my discretion,
Those parts I find most worthy of expression.

She said, "Your promised sails I do not see,   (2518–
And in your word there lies no certainty;   2561)
But I know," she said, "why you treat me thus;
For I was of my love too generous.
And if the gods on which you falsely swore
Will let their vengeance fall on you therefore,
You are not strong enough to bear the pain.
I trusted too much—well may I complain—
In your high lineage and in your fair tongue,
And on the tears that you so falsely wrung."
She said, "How could you weep so cunningly?
Can such true-seeming tears pretended be?
Now, if you will remember what has passed,
There is but little glory on you cast
From having thus an innocent betrayed!
To God," she said, "I pray, and long have prayed,
That it may be your greatest prize of all,
And highest honor that to you shall fall!
And when your ancestors in portraiture
Are seen, so that their honors may endure,
I pray that you be painted there also,
For men to read, as they pass to and fro:
'Lo! this is he, whose flattery betrayed

And caused great woe to an unhappy maid
Who had been true to him in thought and deed!'
But truly, of one point they may yet read,
That you are like your father in this too,
Who was to Ariadne so untrue,
With just such craftiness and subtlety
As you yourself have practiced upon me.
And in that point—although it is not fair—
You follow him, and are his rightful heir.
But since thus sinfully you me beguile,
My body you will see, in a short while,
Come floating into the Athenian bay
Unburied, with no funeral display,
Though you are harder than a stone could be."

This letter she sent to him speedily;
When she found out how brittle and untrue
He had been, in despair herself she slew,
Such grief she had from where she placed her trust.
Women, of this your foe beware you must,
Since even now men may example see;
And trust, where love's concerned, no man but me.

THE LEGEND OF HYPERMNESTRA[62]

In Greece two brothers lived in days of old;
One of them, Danaus, so it is told,
Had sired of sons a number in his day,
As with false lovers often is the way.
There was a single son among the host
Whom Danaus had always loved the most,
And on the morning of his birth proclaimed
That "Lynceus" the baby would be named.
The other brother—Aegyptus was he—
Was false in love as he could wish to be,
And he had many daughters in his life;
Of which he got upon his wedded wife
The youngest, whom he loved best, by his whim,
And Hypermnestra she was named by him.
And this same child, at her nativity,
Was formed for good in every quality;
The gods found pleasing, before she was born,
That of the sheaf she would become the corn.
The Wyrds, whom we think of as Destiny,
Had shaped her so that she would have to be
Merciful, solemn, faithful, modest, good—
All virtues suitable to womanhood.
Venus endowed her with great loveliness;
Jupiter tempered her, nevertheless,
To hold to conscience, truth, and dread of shame,
And in her wifehood to keep her good name—
This, so she thought, was happiness on earth.
Red Mars was at the moment of her birth
So weak that his malicious power failed;
By Venus was his cruel aspect veiled;
Mars, thus restrained by Venus and by all
The other houses, was in might so small
That Hypermnestra dared not touch a knife
With evil thoughts, even to save her life.
Yet—so the heavens did revolve that day
That she fell under Saturn's evil sway,

(2562–
2599)

FIGURE 13. Hypermnestra, from a French translation of *De Claris Mulieribus,* early fifteenth century. By permission of The British Library. Royal Fr16.G.v.f.16v.

And thus she came at last to die in jail,
As I shall narrate later in this tale.[63]

This Danaus and this Aegyptus, though   (2600–
They were two brothers—for, so long ago,   2620)
Close relatives could wed without disgrace—
Decided that a marriage should take place
Of the one's daughter and the other's son
And fixed the day that it should fall upon,
And it was all arranged as they decreed:
The clothing was prepared, time passed with speed;
Soon Lynceus has of his father's brother
The daughter married, and each has the other.
The torches burn, and bright lamps are displayed,
And sacrifices ready to be made;
The burning incense gives off a sweet smell;
The flower is plucked up, and the leaf as well,
To be made into garlands fair to see.
The place is full of sounds of minstrelsy,
And amorous songs of wedding celebration,
All in the custom of that time and nation.
And this took place within Aegyptus' land,
Where everything was done at his command.
And thus the day, into the night, they passed.

Friends took their leave and headed home at last;   (2621–
The night had come, the bride would go to bed.   2646)
Aegyptus then to his own chamber sped,
And that his child be sent for he commanded.
And when at last the guests had all disbanded,
He looked upon his daughter with good cheer,
And spoke to her as you shall shortly hear:
"My dearest daughter, and my heart's chief treasure,
Since first by destiny was made my measure,
Or given by the fatal sisters three,
Nothing has ever been so prized by me
As you, my Hypermnestra, daughter dear.
Take heed of what your father tells you here,
And let one wiser tell you what to do.

So great, my daughter, is my love for you
That all the world means not so much to me.
I would not by my plans do injury
To you, by all that lies beneath the moon.
And what I mean by this will be told soon,
But first there is one warning you must heed:
If you refuse to follow where I lead
You will be dead, by him who rules forever!
In few words I tell you that you will never
Escape my palace safely; you will die
Unless with all my plans you will comply.
Consider this to be my final word."

(2647–
2671)

Poor Hypermnestra quaked at what she heard
As does an aspen leaf, and bowed her head.
Her face took on the pallor of the dead.
She answered, "Lord and father, all your will,
God knows, with all my might I shall fulfill,
Unless it be the cause of my damnation."
"I'll tolerate," he said, "no hesitation";
He took a knife out, like a razor keen.
"Hide this," he said, "so it cannot be seen;
And when your husband is in bed with you,
While he is sleeping, cut his throat in two.
For in my dreams this has been shown to me:
One of my nephews shall my slayer be.
I must take care—I know not which was meant.
Refuse, and we will have an argument,
As I have said, by him I call upon!"
This Hypermnestra's wits were almost gone;
So as to pass unharmed out of that place,
She promised him; there was no other grace.
A bottle then into her hand he pressed,
Saying, "Give to him, when he goes to rest,
A draught, or two, or three, and he will sleep
As long as you would wish it, and as deep,
The opiates and narcotics are so strong.
Now go, lest he find the delay too long."

The bride came forth, with the solemnity (2672–
That in a maiden's face you often see, 2723)
And was led to her room with joy and song.
And shortly, lest this tale should seem too long,
The married pair were quickly brought to bed,
While from that place the others quickly sped.
The night was worn out, and he fell asleep.
With tender feeling she began to weep;
She rose from bed, and with her fear was quaking,
As does the branch which Zephyrus is shaking;
And in the town of Argos all was still.
Then as a frost she felt herself grow chill,
For pity by her heart had seized her so,
And fear of death had made her feel such woe—

Three times she fell down in her sorry case.
Around the chamber she began to pace
And at her hands she gazed down fixedly.
"Alas! with blood shall these hands tainted be?
It does not suit my nature as a maid . . .
My face . . . the clothes in which I am arrayed . . .
My two hands were not made to hold a knife,
Or use it to deprive a man of life.
The devil, what with knives have I to do?
And shall I have my own throat cut in two?
Then I shall bleed, alas! and be undone.
Yet there must be an end to what's begun,
And he or I must surely lose our life.
Now certainly, because I am his wife,
And have my faith, better it is for me
To meet my death in wifely honesty
Than be a traitor living in my shame.
Be as it may, for earnest or for game,
He shall awake, and rise, and go his way,
Along this drainpipe here, before the day."

And she wept tenderly upon his face
And in her arms began him to embrace
And with soft shaking woke him quietly

And through a window he lept speedily
When she had warned him, and had saved him thus.
So swift and light of foot was Lynceus
That from his wife at a great pace he ran.
But she, alas! was weaker than a man,
And helpless, and her flight availed her nought.
Her cruel father saw that she was caught.
Alas! Why, Lynceus, are you unkind?
Why could you not have had it in your mind
To take and lead her with you as you fled?
For when she saw how far he was ahead
And knew she could not run as fast as that,
Nor follow him, then on the ground she sat;
Then she was caught, and into prison led.

For this conclusion has this tale been said

.   .   .   .

["The Legend of Hypermnestra" ends here.]

NOTES TO TRANSLATION

1. This translation is based on *The Works of Geoffrey Chaucer,* 2d ed., ed. Fred N. Robinson (Boston: Houghton Mifflin, 1961).

2. The line numbers in the margins correspond to the line numbers in Robinson's text. The prologue follows his text of the F-version except where indicated in the margin.

3. Probably St. Bernard of Clairvaux.

4. Possible meanings of Middle English *holyday* are modern *holiday, holy day,* or *the holy day,* that is, Sunday.

5. A reference to the love debates apparently popular in medieval courts. Derek Pearsall's edition of *The Floure and the Leaf and The Assembly of Ladies* (1962; reprint ed., Manchester: Manchester University Press, 1980) offers a careful appraisal of the evidence suggesting actual "cults" of the flower and the leaf. Drawing on references in contemporary poetry, he states that apparently "one of the diversions of court society in England and France at the end of the fourteenth century was to divide into two amorous orders, and to argue . . . the comparative merits of the flower and the leaf" (p. 24). He goes on to assert that "no symbolic association was made between the properties of the flower or leaf and the moral qualities of their adherents, though it can readily be seen . . . how natural the moral interpetation was to be" (p. 24). This "moral interpretation" is central to the anonymous poem *The Flower and the Leaf,* which Pearsall places in the late fifteenth century. This dream-vision, attributed to Chaucer in early editions of his works, identifies the leaf with chaste, faithful love, the flower with light love. Its female narrator proclaims herself a humble but devoted adherent of the leaf. The poem's dream-vision form and its theme of chaste love seem to link it closely with the *Legend.* For discussion of this poem and of *The Assembly of Ladies* (its companion in the earliest manuscripts as well as in later editions), see Pearsall's introduction. For discussion of the ideal of chastity as treated in the two poems, see Ann McMillan, "'Fayre Sisters Al': *The Flower and the Leaf* and *The Assembly of Ladies,*" *Tulsa Studies in Women's Literature* 1 (1982): 27–42.

6. The sign of Taurus, the bull. Zeus took the guise of a bull to lure away Agenor's daughter, Europa.

7. "As it would unclose its petals to the rosy-red sun, which on that day [May 1] was in the sign of the Bull [Taurus]."

8. Birds were said to choose their mates on Valentine's Day.

9. A kind of bird.

10. Aristotle's *Ethics*.

11. The confused wording here follows the original.

12. Zephyr, the personified west wind of spring, raped the nymph Chloris, who was then transformed to Flora, goddess of spring.

13. *Daisy* does derive from Anglo-Saxon *day's eye*.

14. Another reference to the love debates of the flower and the leaf. See note 5 above.

15. The following figures are named in Chaucer's *balade*. (Of them, all are women except Absalom and Jonathan. Those whose stories are told in the *Legend* are Lucrece, Cleopatra, Thisbe, Dido, Phyllis, Hypsipyle, Hypermnestra, and Ariadne.) Absalom, King David's son, whose hair caused his death and made him a symbol of beauty; Esther, Jewish heroine; Jonathan, David's friend; Penelope, Ulysses' faithful wife; Marcia, faithful wife of Cato the Younger; Isolde, Tristan's lover; Helen of Troy; Lavinia, Aeneas' wife in Latium; Lucrece, Roman wife who killed herself when she was raped; Polyxena, sacrificed so that she would join Achilles in death; Cleopatra, Mark Antony's lover, a suicide; Thisbe, Pyramus' lover, a suicide; Hero, Leander's lover, a suicide; Laodamia, faithful wife, a suicide; Dido, Aeneas' lover, a suicide; Phyllis, Demophoön's lover, a suicide; Canace, incestuous lover of her brother, put to death by their father; Hypsipyle, Jason's lover; Hypermnestra, who gave her life rather than follow her father's instructions to kill her husband; Ariadne (in Chaucer, Adrian), abandoned by Theseus.

16. Chaucer's word *chere* could mean *appearance* or *expression*.

17. Valerius Maximus praises some women; Titus Livius (Livy) tells Lucrece's story; Claudian writes about the rape of Persephone. For Jerome, see my introduction.

18. Ovid's *Heroides;* see my introduction.

19. Vincent of Beauvais' *Mirror of History*.

20. *The Book of the Duchess*.

21. Included in *The Canterbury Tales* as *The Knight's Tale*.

22. Short poems.

23. Included in *The Canterbury Tales* as *The Second Nun's Tale*.

24. A lost work.

25. Alceste agreed to die in place of her husband, but Hercules rescued her from Hades; see my introduction.

26. A reference to King Richard's royal houses, deleted in the revised prologue; see my introduction.

27. Plato's *Symposium*. It does refer to the story of Alceste (see my introduction), but the "stellification" and transformation into the daisy are apparently Chaucer's inventions.

28. Chaucer's major source for the legend of Cleopatra was probably Boccaccio's *De Claris Mulieribus* or *De Casibus Virorum Illustrium* (see Robinson in Chaucer, *Works*, pp. 846–48). Cleopatra (69–30 B.C.) is the only clearly historical figure in the *Legend*. As was Egyptian royal custom, she married her brother and reigned jointly with him. When he attempted to seize power, Julius Caesar made war on him to restore her to the throne. She was then married to another brother. From 46 to 44 B.C., Cleopatra lived with Julius Caesar in Rome, and she had a son by him. After Caesar's death she returned to Egypt. At that time Mark Antony, Octavian (later Augustus Caesar), and Lepidus were ruling Rome as the Second Triumvirate. Antony had control of Asia and the East. Antony was married to Octavian's sister but deserted her to live in Egypt with Cleopatra, who bore him three children. Angered by Antony's betrayal, Octavian made war on him. Octavian's forces defeated those of Antony and Cleopatra at Actium. Antony, hearing a report of Cleopatra's death, killed himself. Cleopatra tried to win Octavian's sympathy or, by some accounts, to seduce him. Her attempts failed, and she committed suicide by holding a poisonous asp to her breast.

29. Grappling hook, to draw the ship alongside the enemy vessel for boarding.

30. Sickles, to cut the ropes.

31. Poleax and sword are weapons for hand-to-hand combat.

32. Dry peas poured on the deck made the sailors slip and fall.

33. Quicklime thrown into the enemy's eyes would blind him.

34. Thisbe is a figure from Greek mythology. Chaucer's major source is Ovid's *Metamorphoses* (Robinson in Chaucer, *Works*, p. 848). The Babylonian lovers Pyramus and Thisbe grew up in neighbor-

ing houses whose gardens were separated by a wall. Kept apart by their parents, they talked through a small opening in the wall. At last they agreed to elope, arranging to meet at Ninus' tomb. Thisbe, arriving first, was frightened by a lion and dropped her veil, which the lion smeared with blood from a recent kill. Pyramus found the bloody veil and, believing that Thisbe had been killed, stabbed himself. Thisbe then returned, found him dead, and stabbed herself with his sword. Ovid says that blood from their wounds stained the white mulberries red.

35. Legendary virago queen of Babylon.

36. Phoebus Apollo, the sun; Aurora, the dawn.

37. Husband of the mythical queen Semiramis. She is accused of murdering him in some accounts.

38. Dido comes from Roman legend. Chaucer's major sources are Vergil's *Aeneid* and Ovid's *Heroides* (Robinson in Chaucer, *Works*, pp. 848–49). Dido fled to Africa from Phoenicia, where her brother, king of Tyre, had murdered her husband, Sychaeus. There she founded Carthage and ruled it, given independent status by her chaste widowhood. Aeneas, fleeing the fall of Troy, was shipwrecked nearby and made his way to Carthage, where he and Dido became lovers. A message from the gods reminded Aeneas of his destiny to found a kingdom in Italy. Despite Dido's pleas, he left Carthage. Dido stabbed herself with his sword and died cursing him. He later saw her shade among women destroyed by love in the Sorrowing Fields of Hades.

39. Vergil, author of the *Aeneid,* was from Mantua.

40. Sinon was instrumental in the Greek plot of the Trojan horse.

41. Venus, goddess of love, was Aeneas' mother; Anchises, a mortal, his father; Creusa, his wife in Troy; and Ascanius, his son.

42. A neighboring king whose love Dido had spurned. See my introduction.

43. In Robinson, "she." In context, however, "he" (Aeneas) seems the more likely reading.

44. *Heroides.*

45. I.e., you are shown in your true colors.

46. Hypsipyle is a figure from Greek mythology; sources are Ovid's *Metamorphoses* and *Heroides* and Guido delle Colonne's *Historia Troiana* (Robinson in Chaucer, *Works,* pp. 849–50). The women of Lemnos, outraged by their husbands' infidelity, agreed

to kill all the men on the island. Hypsipyle, the king's daughter, helped her father to escape. When Jason and the Argonauts stopped at Lemnos on their way to steal the Golden Fleece, these women welcomed them and used the opportunity to repopulate the island. Hypsipyle was later exiled for having saved her father's life.

47. Guido delle Colonne, author of *Historia Troiana.*

48. The *Argonauticon* of Valerius Flaccus.

49. I.e., Medea. In his telling of her story, Chaucer suppresses Medea's murder of her two children, done to avenge herself on Jason. Hypsipyle's prophetic curse reminds the reader, however.

50. Medea is a favorite figure in Greek mythology. Chaucer's sources are Ovid's *Metamorphoses* and *Heroides* and Guido delle Colonne's *Historia Troiana* (Robinson in Chaucer, *Works,* pp. 849–50). Medea, daughter of the king of Colchis, had great powers of sorcery. Jason and the Argonauts came to Colchis to steal its king's greatest treasure, the Golden Fleece. Medea fell in love with Jason and helped him to obtain the fleece. As they fled aboard his ship, Medea cast parts of her brother's body into the sea so that her father would stop to retrieve them and be delayed in his pursuit. Medea had borne Jason two children when he left her to marry the daughter of a powerful king. Medea sent her a poisoned robe, in which she died a horrible death. Medea then avenged herself further on Jason by killing their children. She escaped in a chariot drawn by dragons.

51. A stock term, but Medea, a sorceress, was learned in witchcraft.

52. Lucrece is a figure from Roman legend. Chaucer's source is Ovid's *Fasti.* Lucrece (or Lucretia) was a Roman wife of high standing who was raped by the son of king Tarquinius Superbus ("the proud"). She made public the dishonor he had done to her, then killed herself. The outcry was so great that Tarquin was overthrown and the kingship replaced by the system of elected consuls.

53. The Roman historian Livy is cited as an "authority" but does not appear to have been used as a source. See Robinson's comment in Chaucer, *Works,* p. 850.

54. Ariadne and Phaedra are Greek mythological figures. Major sources for Chaucer's version are Ovid's *Metamorphoses* and *Heroides.* Ariadne and Phaedra were daughters of Minos, king of

Crete. Ariadne (but here Phaedra is responsible for the plan) thwarted her father by enabling Theseus to kill the Minotaur, a monster to which Theseus had been sent as a sacrifice. Ariadne provided Theseus with a ball of thread that enabled him to find his way back through the Labyrinth made for the beast. Theseus abandoned Ariadne on an island, where the god Dionysus found her and married her. Phaedra later became Theseus' wife. She fell in love with his son Hippolytus. When he spurned her she killed herself, leaving a message that Hippolytus had tried to rape her. Theseus pronounced a fatal curse on his son; later Theseus learned his mistake and was stricken with remorse.

55. Nisus' daughter Scylla fell in love with Minos and aided him by cutting off her father's magical lock of hair. See Robinson's comment in Chaucer, *Works*, p. 851.

56. The Minotaur, for which Daedalus designed the Labyrinth. This monster—half man, half bull—was the offspring of Minos' queen, Pasiphae, who indulged in unnatural lust for a bull.

57. I.e., Ariadne responded to his words and to his appearance.

58. Ariadne's Crown is not "in the sign of Taurus" but is a different constellation, the Corona Borealis. Robinson (Chaucer, *Works*, p. 851) suggests that Chaucer may have meant that this constellation can be seen most easily when the sun is in the sign of Taurus.

59. Philomela and Procne come from Greek mythology. Chaucer's major sources are Ovid's *Metamorphoses* and the *Ovide Moralisé* (Robinson's comment in Chaucer, *Works*, pp. 852–53). Tereus married Procne; later he abducted and raped her sister Philomela, cutting out her tongue so that she could not reveal the truth. Philomela wove the story into a length of cloth and sent it to Procne. Enraged, Procne killed her son and served his flesh to his father Tereus. The gods changed them into birds: Tereus into the hoopoe, Procne into the swallow, and Philomela into the nightingale.

60. Phyllis comes from Greek mythology. Chaucer's source is Ovid's *Heroides* (Robinson in Chaucer, *Works*, pp. 853). Phyllis, queen of Thrace, became the lover of Theseus' son Demophoön, who was shipwrecked on her shores. He left her to return to Athens, promising to return within a certain time and marry her. When he failed to return within the stated time, she hanged herself, repenting her unchastity.

61. These proverbs of foxes and ducks emphasize inherited instinct as the cause of behavior.

62. Hypermnestra comes from Greek mythology; Chaucer's source is Ovid's *Heroides* (Robinson in Chaucer, *Works,* pp. 853–54). Danaus had fifty daughters; his brother Aegyptus had fifty sons. Danaus, fearing a prophecy that one of his nephews would kill him, allowed a marriage between them and his daughters. He then ordered all his daughters to kill their husbands on their wedding night. All obeyed except Hypermnestra, who arranged for her husband to escape. She was captured and put to death by her father, who was later killed by the nephew whom she had saved.

63. This astrological passage, original with Chaucer, shows Hypermnestra to have been predestined from the moment of her conception to be unable to use a knife, even in self-defense.

SUGGESTIONS FOR FURTHER READING

I. SELECTED WORKS ON MEDIEVAL WOMEN

Bridenthal, Renate, and Koonz, Claudia, eds. *Becoming Visible: Women in European History*. Boston: Houghton Mifflin, 1977. Twenty essays by various writers embrace the whole history of women, from prehistoric past to envisioned future. Chapters on medieval women are "Sanctity and Power: The Dual Pursuit of Medieval Women," by Jo Ann McNamara and Suzanne F. Wemple; and "The Pedestal and the Stake: Courtly Love and Witchcraft," by E. William Monter. "Sanctity and Power" discusses the "duality of the Christian tradition regarding women: negative perceptions of female nature mandated their subordinate role in ritual, yet theology proclaimed the spiritual equality of all believers" (p. 90). The authors conclude that "women of the high and late Middle Ages (1100–1500) found their rights and roles increasingly curtailed and their ambitions frustrated" (p. 117). Monter's essay offers a suggestive parallel between the apparently opposed medieval portrayals of women as angelic or demonic. Even the witch, he argues, plays a passive role, destructive "only because she has been unable to resist . . . the devil" (p. 119). Testimony and statistics from witch trials dramatize the fact that this form of misogyny "provided a legal method for killing dozens of thousands of women" (p. 133).

Davis, Natalie Zemon. *Society and Culture in Early Modern France*. Stanford: Stanford University Press, 1975. This volume of essays focuses on the fifteenth to eighteenth centuries but contains useful insights into earlier periods. Chapter Five, "Women on Top," is a lively illustration of the fact that "the female sex . . . was thought the disorderly one par excellence in early modern Europe" (p. 124). This "disorderliness was founded in physiology" (p. 124); woman was believed ruled by her uterus, "fragile and unsteady" (p. 125). Davis discusses the societal use of "sexual inversion"—that is, switches in sex roles—as "a widespread form of cultural play in literature, in art, and in festivity" (p. 129). One form of this inversion focused on the unruly woman and served as "an expression of, and an outlet for, conflicts about authority within the system; and . . . also provided occasions by which the authoritarian current . . . could be moderated by the laughter of discord and paradoxical play" (p. 142). Analogies with Chaucer's Wife of Bath and perhaps even the *Legend*'s inverted "good women" are unmistakable.

Delany, Sheila. *Writing Woman: Women Writers and Women in Literature, Medieval to Modern*. New York: Schocken Books, 1983. In ten essays, Delany explores "the literary use of sexual behavior as an image of political behavior" (p. 17). Relevant essays are "*Flore et Jehan:* The Bourgeois Woman in Medieval Life and Letters"; "Womanliness in *The Man of Law's Tale*"; "Slaying Python: Marriage and Misogyny in a Chaucerian Text"; "Sexual Economics, Chaucer's Wife of Bath, and *The Book of Margery Kempe*"; and "A City, a Room: The Scene of Writing in Christine de Pisan and Virginia Woolf." Delany discusses the workings of class and culture upon authors and characters. In "Slaying Python," particularly, she shows her impatience with critics who dismiss antifeminism in Chaucer's works as attributable to narrator or character rather than to the poet himself. This essay also includes a very suggestive discussion of the psychological roots of misogyny (see especially pp. 59–75). Likewise, Delany sees in the Wife of Bath Chaucer's condemnation of "the competitive, accumulative practices of the medieval bourgeoisie" (p. 79) and judges the Wife's rebellion against her society to be partial and failed. The essay on Virginia Woolf and Christine de Pizan offers moving personal testimony to these writers, so distant from one another in time and so tragically close in situation. Her discussion of *The City of Ladies* (pp. 188–90) explicates Christine's motives and techniques in "rewriting woman good."

Diamond, Arlyn, and Edwards, Lee R., eds. *The Authority of Experience: Essays in Feminist Criticism*. Amherst: University of Massachusetts Press, 1977. Two essays are relevant: Maureen Fries, "'Slydynge of Corage': Chaucer's Criseyde as Feminist and Victim," and Arlyn Diamond, "Chaucer's Women and Women's Chaucer." Fries discusses Criseyde's position in light of marriage laws governing relations between men and women and judges that "in this context, Criseyde's desire for freedom is a sensible one" (p. 48). Fries concludes that Criseyde cannot achieve this freedom because "she cannot do without male protection. . . . Inculturated with all the virtues—tenderness, modesty, submissiveness, forgiveness, and above all beauty and amiability—expected from a person of her sex, time, and class, she cannot

escape" (p. 57). Diamond's essay is "an examination of Chaucer inspired by feminist concerns" (p. 60). The essay discusses the so-called
Marriage Group, especially *The Wife of Bath's Tale*. Diamond argues
that "intelligence, energy, and drive are all words appropriate to her,
and they ought to be attractive, but when they are attached to a female
they become threatening, hence Chaucer has transmuted her potential
for genuine female strength into a constellation of fantasies and attributes which have been defined as the 'aggressive female'" (p. 69).
Diamond concludes that Chaucer "can pity women, he can see some
way into them, and make us see how often distorting the conventional
sex roles are, but we want more from him, perhaps because he has already given so much" (p. 83).

Ferrante, Joan M. "The Education of Women in the Middle Ages in
Theory, Fact, and Fantasy." In *Beyond Their Sex: Learned Women of
the European Past,* ed. Patricia H. Labalme, pp. 9–42. New York:
New York University Press, 1980. Ferrante gives an overview of women's
education in the medieval period, focusing especially on the twelfth
century as offering what was, relatively speaking, a golden age for
learned women. She discusses three outstanding women intellectuals
from that century: Heloise, Hildegard of Bingen, and Marie de France.
The twelfth century, Ferrante demonstrates, also witnessed the addi-
tion of education and wisdom to the desirable attributes of romance
heroines. In the twelfth century, she concludes, "the educated woman
. . . can command the respect and attention of the male establishment,
and the educated heroine . . . can elicit the sympathy of the audience"
(pp. 34–35).

———. *Woman as Image in Medieval Literature: From the Twelfth
Century to Dante.* New York: Columbia University Press, 1975. Chapters discuss images of women in biblical exegesis, allegory, courtly
literature, the literature of the thirteenth century, and Dante. This brief
volume offers very useful discussions of works that are often antholo-
gized today together with works that are seldom read except by scholars in the field. Its observations are imaginative and important far beyond the bounds of its particular subjects. For example, one can find
many applications for her observation that the heroines in Thomas's
Tristan "are differentiated only by the degree to which they reflect
[Tristan's] image" (p. 94).

Harksen, Sibylle. *Women in the Middle Ages.* Trans. Marianne Herz-
feld, rev. George A. Shepperson. New York: Abner Schram, 1975.

Chapters discuss "Women's Rights in Medieval Law," "Life in Castles, Towns and Villages," "Women at Work," "Saints, Nuns and Heretics," "Women in Positions of Power," "Art and Music," and "Literature." Artistic representations of women from the tenth through the fifteenth centuries are grouped and discussed under these headings. The illustrations reveal many details of women's lives, from childbirth practices to burial customs, together with the images—idealized and demonic—that surrounded and shaped those lives.

Lucas, Angela M. *Women in the Middle Ages: Religion, Marriage and Letters.* Brighton, Eng.: Harvester Press, 1983. Lucas's study focuses chiefly on English women from the fifth through the fifteenth centuries and relates "women's role in literature to ideas prevailing in the society" (p. xi). She includes legal, theological, and medical documents, sermons, and the like. The first section, on religion, offers extensive documentation from primary sources on the importance of virginity for women. In her section on marriage, Lucas offers a useful summary of some of the theories governing that institution. For example, she explains that the fear and dread surrounding sexual intercourse became linked in the thirteenth century with "the new study of Aristotle, for whom rationalism and contemplation were to be valued above all else. Sexual orgasm, because it momentarily overcomes rational thought, made many respected writers . . . extremely nervous about the rightness of such pleasure" (p. 114). In "Women and Letters," Lucas discusses Christine de Pizan, Hildegard of Bingen, Heloise, the Paston women, Elizabeth of Shonau, Margery Kempe, Hrotswitha, Julian of Norwich, Marie de France, and others in terms of what is known of their lives and education. Lucas's bibliography is particularly useful as a listing of relevant primary sources in their currently available editions.

Power, Eileen. *Medieval Women,* ed. M. M. Postan. Cambridge, Eng.: Cambridge University Press, 1975. A preface; chapters on medieval ideas about women, the lady, working women, education, and nunneries; and well-integrated illustrations make this brief volume (just over a hundred pages) an especially useful introduction to the subject. Power is careful to point out that "the position of women is one thing in theory, another in legal position, yet another in everyday life. In the Middle Ages, as now, the various manifestations of women's position reacted on one another but did not exactly coincide; the true position of women was a blend of all three" (p. 9).

Shahar, Shulamith. *The Fourth Estate: A History of Women in the Middle Ages.* Trans. Chaya Galai. London: Methuen Publishers, 1983. Shahar's study focuses chiefly on the High and Late Middle Ages (early twelfth through mid-fifteenth centuries) in Western Europe. Chapters discuss "Public and Legal Rights," "Nuns," "Married Women," "Women in the Nobility," "Townswomen," "Women in the Peasantry," and "Witches and the Heretical Movements." Shahar is especially interested in women's involvement in heretical movements, "in which they enjoyed higher status and wider rights than in the Roman Catholic Church, and were also somewhat freer of male domination, although the improvement of the status of women was not a particular object of any of these movements" (p. 9). The Waldenses and Cathars receive particular attention. In the latter group, women were allowed to become "Perfects" and, as such, to "preach, bless, and administer the *consolamentum*" (p. 259). Yet the group "minimized the function of the Holy Mother" (p. 260) while "[retaining] . . . the image of woman as the temptress and corrupter who is also a creature inferior to man" (p. 261). Her discussion of the preponderance of women among those accused of witchcraft (pp. 277–80) includes a brief summary of the antifeminist tradition and its psychological roots.

Warner, Marina. *Joan of Arc: The Image of Female Heroism.* New York: Alfred A. Knopf, 1981. This volume sets a standard for historical writing in its careful examination both of the historical Joan and of the images that grew up around her in her lifetime and survive, with many permutations, to the present day. Like Warner's earlier work *Alone of All Her Sex: The Myth and Cult of the Virgin Mary, Joan of Arc* shows how the images and ideals attached to women in different times reveal the values and assumptions of those times. As Warner says, "Joan was an individual in history and real time, but she is also the protagonist of a famous story in the timeless dimension of myth, and the way that story has come to be told tells yet another story, one about our concept of the heroic, the good and the pure" (p. 7). Joan, she further argues, "has extended the taxonomy of female types. . . . [She] illuminates the operation of our present classification system, its rigidity on the one hand, its potential on the other" (p. 9).

Weissman, Hope Phyllis. "Antifeminism and Chaucer's Characterizations of Women." In *Geoffrey Chaucer,* ed. George D. Economou, pp. 93–110. New York: McGraw-Hill Publishers, 1975. Weissman points out that antifeminist literature includes not only that which presents woman "as a nagging bully and an avaricious whore" but also "any presentation of a woman's nature intended to conform her to male expectations of what she is or ought to be, not her own" (p. 94). She discusses many of the *Canterbury Tales* in terms of these images. "The Wife of Bath," Weissman argues, "is most truly the feminist in her effort to dispense with images of women altogether . . . but [she] is also imprisoned by the antifeminism of her culture, for at her tale's conclusion the image becomes her will" (p. 105).

Wilson, Katharina M., ed. *Medieval Women Writers*. Athens: University of Georgia Press, 1984. This volume contains fifteen essays designed to "introduce the reader to some of the outstanding women writers of the Middle Ages." Noted critics represented include Joan Ferrante, Peter Dronke, and Charity Cannon Willard. Famous figures such as Hrotsvit (Hrotswitha), Heloise, and Hildegard appear together with lesser-known writers. These figures range in time from the ninth through the fifteenth centuries and include ten regions or nationalities (Frankish, Saxon, Brabantian, French, English, Spanish, Swedish, Occitanian, German, and Italian). The collection is intended as an introduction for students and general readers; many of the contributing authors have articles and volumes in print or in progress that discuss these women in greater detail. This collection's strength is its inclusiveness. A brief introductory essay by the editor draws some useful parallels and distinctions among the individual women and between the women as a group and the male authors who were their contemporaries.

Women's Studies 11 (1984), nos. 1 and 2. Hope Phyllis Weissman is general editor of this volume devoted to medieval women. Essays include Jo Ann McNamara, "Cornelia's Daughters: Paula and Eustochium"; Linda Seidel, "Salome and the Canons"; Joan M. Ferrante, "Male Fantasy and Female Reality in Courtly Literature"; Clifford Davidson, "Women and the Medieval Stage"; Heath Dillard, "Medieval Women in Castilian Town Communities"; Rodney H. Hilton, "Women Traders in Medieval England"; H. Marshall Leicester, Jr., "Of a Fire in the Dark: Public and Private Feminism in the *Wife of Bath's Tale*"; and Caroline Walker Bynum, "Women Mystics and Eucharistic Devotion in the Thirteenth Century." As one might expect, this collection is especially concerned with integrating medieval studies and feminist concerns. McNamara's article, for example, offers a careful critique of St. Jerome's teachings aimed at women and of the actual women who formed his "circle." She questions the assumption that, in following what are now held to be antifeminist teachings about hatred of the body, these women were not making a defensible choice in their own terms. She argues that they may not have been brainwashed victims—as they are often depicted today—but followers of an ideal that freed them from many of the constraints that would otherwise have been their lot. Ferrante's essay shows that even in the literature of courtly love women were not voiceless, as is often supposed; women did compose in the courtly love tradition and genres, and their works often take issue with the simplistic treatments of women and love found in the works of contemporary male authors.

II. SELECTED WORKS ON THE LEGEND OF GOOD WOMEN SINCE 1960

Delany, Sheila. In two essays (unpublished at this writing), Delany explores Chaucer's use of obscene wordplay in the *Legend*. In "The Naked Text: Chaucer's 'Thisbe,' the *Ovide Moralisé,* and the Problem of *Translatio Studii*," she argues that the presence of obscene wordplay in the legend of Thisbe shows Chaucer's use of the *Ovide Moralisé* to be more extensive than usually thought. In "The Logic of Obscenity in Chaucer's *Legend of Good Women*," obscenity is used, Delany says, to undermine "the reductive propagandistic task laid on the poet by the God of Love" (p. 2). Obscenity also "helps to re-establish . . . a more accurate, balanced and 'natural' view of women than could be provided either by courtly love or by its inverse, clerical misogyny" (pp. 2–3).

Frank, Robert Worth, Jr. *Chaucer and The Legend of Good Women.* Cambridge, Mass.: Harvard University Press, 1972. Frank opens his discussion of the *Legend* by focusing on 1386—the assumed year of its inception—as a "period . . . of change and . . . of crisis" (p. 2) for the poet, who "is now intensely interested in narrative, in stories—as many of them as possible" (p. 10). Frank therefore sees the *Legend* as an exercise in narrative style, especially in abbreviation. He views the religious and amorous imagery of the prologue as "deliberately misleading" (p. 12), Chaucer's real intent being "to tell a series of tales . . . for their own sake" (p. 14). Frank sees little importance in the avowed purpose of the *Legend:* "all that his stories will 'prove' is that particular women, and by implication many women, are faithful" (p. 17). Although he observes that "there are playful overtones to this dictum throughout" (p. 17), Frank believes that the legends "were to be presented as stories of real events occurring in the past" (p. 21). Chaucer could succeed in this attempt at historicity, Frank argues, because the stories were "strange" (p. 21) and unfamiliar to their readers. Frank, focusing as he does on narrative techniques and their relative success in the various legends, makes finer distinctions among the legends than do most critics. For example, he has high praise for Chaucer's skill at manipulating his material for unified effect in the story of Hypermnestra, but he judges the story of Dido a qualified success and that of Cleopatra a failure.

Fyler, John M. *Chaucer and Ovid.* New Haven: Yale University Press, 1979. Fyler's fourth chapter, "The *Legend of Good Women*: Palinode and Procrustean Bed," offers a concise, well-written, and wise reading of the *Legend* as "a wonderfully comic exercise in censorship and distorted emphasis" (p. 99). Fyler draws upon Leach's discussion of the *Legend* to argue that "the cumulative effect of Chaucer's deletions is compelling: we cannot avoid recognizing a consistent pattern of censorship" (p. 99). He points out that "usually the preconceived pattern of sanctity defeats its own intent by enervating female heroism" (p. 107); a footnote contrasts Chaucer's method with "the extreme view of Boccaccio, in *De Mulieribus Claris,* where the good woman is essentially a man." Finally, Fyler says, this "attempt to find *trouthe* where there is none does not . . . accomplish very much" (p. 123). Of greatest significance in the *Legend* are the truths pointed up by their absence: "the *Legend* and *Troilus* together reveal that the difference between an ironic narrowing of the poet's vision and the poet with his powers fully extended is insignificant compared to the gulf between either and the heavenly perspective we accept by faith but cannot attain on earth" (p. 115).

Hansen, Elaine Tuttle. "Irony and the Antifeminist Narrator in Chaucer's *Legend of Good Women*." *Journal of English and Germanic Philology* 82 (1983): 11–31. Hansen's views on the *Legend*'s irony are similar to those of Eleanor Leach and John Fyler, but she focuses on the Chaucerian narrator—along with Cupid and the antifeminist tradition—as a primary object of satire. She argues that the narrator (though not Chaucer himself) "identifies with his own gender and is much more concerned with men and their affairs than with women, good or bad" (p. 20). Hansen also entertains, but rejects, the possibility that I find more persuasive: that the narrator "is poking fun at Cupid by giving him a poem whose effect is exactly the opposite of what the god ordered" (p. 28). The good woman "is victimized if she follows the rules of Love and lives up to feminine ideals; unworthy, unloved, and unsung if she does not" (p. 28).

Kiser, Lisa J. *Telling Classical Tales: Chaucer and the Legend of Good Women.* Ithaca, N.Y.: Cornell University Press, 1983. Kiser argues that "the *Legend*'s ostensible subject, love, is not its real subject at all. Rather, the poem was written to set forth some of Chaucer's basic views about literature: its sources, its usefulness, its forms, its audience, and its capacity to represent Christian truth" (p. 9). With this interpretation in mind, Kiser discusses medieval theories of literature and Chaucer's understanding and use of them—especially metaphor (Chapter 2), *exemplum* (Chapter 3), and the medieval literary terms "poesy," "makyng," and "translacioun" (Chapter 5). Chapter 4 analyzes the conflict between the *Legend*'s classical sources and its medieval hagiographic treatment of them. Kiser concludes that the *Legend,* while "clearly existing primarily to describe and defend Chaucer's principles of classical storytelling as they had appeared in the *Troilus,* must also be viewed as a poem about metaphor, poetry's dependence on metaphor, the nature of poetic abstraction, the problems caused by readers' misunderstandings, the relation of Christian truth to secular art, translation, and the relative merits of experience and authority in our quest for knowledge" (p. 151).

Kolve, V. A. "From Cleopatra to Alceste: An Iconographic Study of *The Legend of Good Women.*" In *Signs and Symbols in Chaucer's Poetry,* ed. John P. Hermann and John J. Burke, Jr., pp. 130–78. University, Ala.: University of Alabama Press, 1977. Kolve uses a close reading of possible sources for Chaucer's Cleopatra and Alceste, plus examinations of *memento mori* and other art, to read the *Legend* "iconographically and with an exercise of the historical imagination" (p. 146). He argues that Chaucer alters accounts of Cleopatra's death so that she "dramatizes . . . the medieval commonplace that man's flesh was eaten by worms and serpents in the grave" (p. 146). Her fate is echoed in the fates of the other good women, whose stories likewise end in doom and futility, if not fatality. Kolve asserts that Chaucer, while admiring his good women's courage and virtue, nevertheless shows that, as pagans, "their deaths and their suffering address no values higher than fame, the avoidance of shame, the preservation of a good name" (p. 151). The reiterated hopelessness of their stories is redeemed for Kolve by Chaucer's unrealized intention to end his poem with the legend of Alceste: "he was moving steadily toward the legend of a death that had served an end beyond its own fame: the legend of a lover willing to die so that another might live, and who earned her own release from death thereby" (p. 171). Alceste "adumbrates the redemptive history of Christ" (p. 173); "her body does not feed the worms, and her destiny transcends the grave" (p. 178).

Leach, Eleanor Winsor. "The Sources and Rhetoric of Chaucer's 'Legend of Good Women' and Ovid's 'Heroides.'" Ph.D. diss., Yale University, 1963. Leach's unpublished dissertation is referred to throughout this work. Her discussion of the *Legend* and its most important source, the *Heroides,* is extremely useful in the information it provides and suggestive in the interpretation it offers. Particularly important is her second chapter, "Convention and Rhetoric," in which she discusses Chaucer's use of abbreviation (pp. 62–75) and amplification (pp. 76–92) under the heading, "Rhetoric as a System." In "Rhetoric as Proof: The Legends and their Sources," she discusses Chaucer's uses of and references to authority (see especially pp. 101–117, Cleopatra; 118–30, Lucrece; 149–65, Dido). A useful summary is provided in pages 205–211. Leach's work is seminal to any reading of the *Legend* in terms of its avowed purpose—the praise of women who suffered for love.

Overbeck, Pat Trefzger. "Chaucer's Good Woman." *Chaucer Review* 2 (1967): 75–94. Overbeck's article plays a formative role in my own reading of the *Legend.* The article argues that, "having accepted Love's commission [to follow the authority of old books and of the God himself] . . . Chaucer . . . juggles his sources to produce his Good Woman, the woman who cannot or will not relate to authority, the consummate woman of experience" (p. 76). "Alienated from divine authority" and "reject[ing] human authority" (p. 78), "his queens [believe that] the only meaningful sovereignty is in the love relationship" (p. 78). Mere passion will not satisfy her; she wants marriage, and she gives up everything for it. "The prototypal Good Woman, free from the restraints of authority and the dictates of reason, pursues an *ignis fatuus,* a hallowed earthly union or a sublunary perfection impossible of attainment, destroying herself in the process" (p. 85). Overbeck draws suggestive parallels among the good women of the legends and Chaucer's other "good women," especially the Wife of Bath.

Taylor, Beverly. "The Medieval Cleopatra: The Classical and Medieval Tradition of Chaucer's *Legend of Cleopatra*." *Journal of Medieval and Renaissance Studies* 7 (1977): 249–69. Taylor shows that "writings about Cleopatra in classical antiquity consistently reveal her flaunting a variety of vices and condemn her for the widespread destruction she caused" (p. 253). Moreover, "if anything, the medieval Cleopatra was less esteemed than her classical antecedent" (p. 253). Dante, Petrarch, and Boccaccio treat her as an emblem of lust and cruelty. Gower and Chaucer himself, in *The Parliament of Fowls,* include her among those "noted for incest, for adultery, and . . . for following love to destruction" (p. 259). Taylor concludes that Chaucer's legend of Cleopatra is "a highly ironic and condemnatory portrait" (p. 269) that "provides [a context] for the following tales in the *Legend of Good Women*" (p. 269).

Wasserman, Julian N., and Blanch, Robert N., eds. *Chaucer in the Eighties*. Syracuse, N.Y.: Syracuse University Press, 1986. This volume of selected papers from the second "Chaucer at Albany" conference contains three essays on the *Legend*. Ruth M. Ames, in "The Feminist Connections of Chaucer's *Legend of Good Women*" (pp. 57–73), places the *Legend* in the context of the literary argument over the *Romance of the Rose*. She argues that this "controversy . . . is a direct influence on the *Legend*" (p. 62). Sheila Delany, in "Rewriting Women Good: Gender and the Anxiety of Influence in Two Late-Medieval Texts," contrasts the *Legend* with Christine's *Cité des Dames* as poetic encounters with the medieval antifeminist tradition. "Both works purport to rewrite that tradition in order to present a new image of woman . . . [as] courageous and loyal, prudent and kind" (p. 76). Christine succeeds, in her view, while Chaucer does not. Chaucer deliberately undermines the false ideal portrayed by the women of the legends; however, he also—unintentionally—undermines the true ideal that he attempts to portray in Alceste. Despite his efforts to make her an efficacious heroine, Delany says, Alceste remains Object and Other. Russell A. Peck's "Chaucerian Poetics and the Prologue to the *Legend of Good Women*" (pp. 39–55) discusses the figures of Cupid and Alceste as representing the forces of nature and "natural piety" governing Chaucer's poetics.

INDEX